"No one leaves until I give the order," said U.S. Army Captain Jean Philipe Thibodeaux.

The sergeant nodded. "Yes, sir."

Footsteps sounded to Phil's left. He turned and spotted Agent Jamison Steele walking purposefully toward him. If Jamison had been assigned to investigate the training incident, Phil could breathe a sigh of relief.

Phil turned to the CID agent. "You've been assigned the case?"

"Negative. I'm here to secure the range and assist Major Hansen." Jamison looked over his shoulder toward the bleacher area. "Special Agent Kelly McQueen will be handling this one."

Phil's heart thumped against his chest as he followed Jamison's gaze and recognized the very determined complication walking toward them.

A number of guys called her the Ice McQueen. That, coupled with the fact that she'd won the Outstanding Marksmanship Award, was off-putting to some.

Biting down on his jaw, he steeled himself to the ironic twist of events. Phil didn't need the Ice McQueen in his life. No matter how attracted he was to her.

Books by Debby Giusti

Love Inspired Suspense

Nowhere to Hide
Scared to Death
MIA: Missing in Atlanta
*Countdown to Death
*Protecting Her Child
Christmas Peril
  "Yule Die"
Killer Headline
†The Officer's Secret
†The Captain's Mission

*Magnolia Medical
†Military Investigations

DEBBY GIUSTI

is a medical technologist who loves working with test tubes and petri dishes almost as much as she loves to write. Growing up as an army brat, Debby met and married her husband—then a captain in the army—at Fort Knox, Kentucky. Together they traveled the world, raised three wonderful army brats of their own and have now settled in Atlanta, Georgia, where Debby spins tales of suspense that touch the heart and soul. Contact Debby through her website, www.DebbyGiusti.com, email debby@debbygiusti.com, or write c/o Love Inspired Suspense, 233 Broadway, Suite 1001 New York, NY 10279.

The Captain's Mission

Debby Giusti

Love Inspired

Recycling programs
for this product may
not exist in your area.

LOVE INSPIRED BOOKS

ISBN-13: 978-0-373-44461-8

THE CAPTAIN'S MISSION

Copyright © 2011 by Deborah W. Giusti

www.LoveInspiredBooks.com

Printed in U.S.A.

The thief comes only to steal and kill and destroy;
I have come that they may have life,
and have it to the full.
—*John* 10:10

This book is dedicated to
our brave men and women in uniform,
to Jesus who inspires me,
to my family who loves me,
to the Seekers who support me.

Thank you to my editor Emily Rodmell
and my agent Deidre Knight.

ONE

"Cease fire!" U.S. Army Captain Jean Philippe Thibodeaux screamed into the handheld radio microphone from inside his Bradley Fighting Vehicle. The order echoed back to him as the "cease fire" was relayed across the live-fire range to the three platoons involved in the training exercise at Fort Rickman, Georgia.

Under Phil's command, his two-hundred-man company of soldiers had advanced on a series of targets representing enemy strongholds. The men had maneuvered for nearly an hour, firing live rounds that ripped through the cardboard facsimiles of enemy soldiers while the unit's heavier weapons shot at mock-ups of armored personnel carriers and enemy tanks. The mission had gone like clockwork with nary a glitch, but only minutes before the completion of the exercise everything had come to an unexpected halt.

Heart hammering in his chest, Phil leaped from the Bradley from which he had led the attack and ran toward the small rise on the so-called battlefield where a group of men clustered. Behind him, the executive officer and First Sergeant Jerry Meyers followed Phil's lead.

A frenzy of activity erupted as men exited their vehicles. Foot soldiers stopped their forward advancement and looked around as if trying to find a reason why the attack had been halted.

In the distance, a field ambulance raced along the rugged terrain and screeched to a stop near the small rise. A team of medics disappeared into the sea of camouflage uniforms that had gathered.

Moments earlier, the blasts of 25-millimeter chain guns and the staccato fire of the M-4 carbines had filled the February evening in a mounting crescendo until the captain's order halted the Bradleys and suspended the battle.

The governor of the State of Georgia and his entourage as well as military personnel from post and a select group of local civilians had watched from the reviewing stands and bleachers as C Company, Second Battalion, Fifteenth Infantry—Phil's company—had advanced on the targets.

One face had stood out from the crowd. Special Agent Kelly McQueen was blonde and blue-eyed and had been assigned to guard the visiting dignitaries. Along with the military police, Agent McQueen was, no doubt, currently directing the VIPs out of the reviewing stands and escorting them into vans parked by the roadway. Without delay, she would escort them to the airfield on post where a plane waited to fly them back to Atlanta.

In similar fashion, the crowd of onlookers in the bleachers would be herded aboard buses for transport back to the main post area. Every effort was being made to maintain calm and order. No one wanted panic to ensue or to alert the public that anything out of the ordinary had occurred. The falling darkness and mass of soldiers gathered around the incident site would keep curious eyes at bay.

God willing, no one would realize the magnitude of the problem downrange. Not that Phil would count on the Lord. After everything that had happened in his childhood, he had vowed long ago to make his own way in life.

To this day, he refused to acknowledge a so-called loving God who allowed his father to go to prison and his mother to care more about her career than her twelve-year-old son whose world had come crashing down around him.

The same feelings he'd had as a young boy were bubbling up within him now. What had gone wrong?

Phil increased his speed, ignoring the dust stirred up by the Bradleys that had rumbled across the range. The smell of cordite and smoke, produced from the exploding rounds, mixed with the dirt-clogged air and hovered over the range, painting the desolate terrain in an eerie veil of gloom.

Nearing the crest of the rise, he pushed through the throng of soldiers that had taken part in the training mission. They now stared with wide eyes and drawn faces at the medics who feverishly tried to bring the soldier back to life.

Phil's gut constricted as his eyes focused on Corporal Rick Taylor, First Platoon. The medics had removed the outer tactical vest that had protected Taylor's chest but not his groin, where a bullet had ripped through his flesh. Blood—too much blood—soaked through his uniform and mixed with the red Georgia clay. One of the medics jammed a handful of gauze squares into the open wound, stopping the flow of blood as a second man pushed down on Taylor's sternum. A third cut through the sleeve of his uniform and searched for a vein.

The trio worked feverishly, but Taylor's limp body failed to respond. Eventually, the medics sat back on their haunches and shook their heads. The leader of the team turned doleful eyes to Phil. "There's nothing more we can do."

"You can continue CPR," Phil demanded. A mix of anger and determination swelled within him.

"It's useless, sir."

Their refusal to follow his command frustrated Phil. He shoved them aside and dropped to his knees beside the fallen soldier. Fisting his own hands, he pushed down on Taylor's chest.

"Sir, please." One of the medics tugged on Phil's sleeve.

He jerked his arm away. "I won't let him die."

The gathering of soldiers pressed in even closer. Phil glanced up at his first sergeant. "Clear the area."

"Yes, sir." Jerry Meyers raised his voice. "You heard Captain Thibodeaux, let's move it."

The men—officers, noncommissioned officers and enlisted men—backed away from the death scene and lumbered toward the edge of the range.

A second medic attempted to pull Phil away from the fallen soldier. "He's gone, sir."

Twisting out of the soldier's hold, Phil blew two quick breaths into Corporal Taylor's mouth. He hadn't lost a man in Afghanistan. He would do everything in his power to ensure he didn't lose a soldier stateside.

"Sir, please."

Once again, Phil interlaced his fingers and pushed down on Taylor's chest as he continued to count. "And one and two and…"

Someone knelt in the dirt next to him. A heavy hand rested on his shoulder. "Phil, it's over. You've got to stop."

He glanced up to see his battalion commander's face lined with concern.

"You hear me, son?"

"But, sir—"

Lieutenant Colonel Ken Knowlton—tall and lanky, with a pointed nose and penetrating eyes—placed his hands firmly over Phil's doubled fists and lifted them off the fallen soldier's chest. "You tried your best, Captain. The good Lord called Corporal Taylor home."

Phil jerked out of his hold just as he had done with the medics.

"Listen to me, Phil. You've got to stop. It's over. There's nothing you can do to bring him back."

His commander's voice was firm, and his words cut like a knife into Phil's heart. As much as he didn't want to comply, Lieutenant Colonel Knowlton was right.

A lump clogged Phil's throat, and his eyes blurred. He blinked to clear his vision and focused on Taylor's ashen face.

Knowlton's hand on Phil's elbow encouraged him to stand. Struggling to his feet, he turned his gaze to the thick patch of tall pine trees that rimmed the edge of the training range. He didn't want anyone, especially his battalion commander, to see the moisture that stung his eyes.

He swallowed down the mass of burning bile that had risen from his stomach and, with clenched jaw and sheer determination, turned back to his commander. "I…I can assure you, sir, I'll get to the bottom of this."

Knowlton nodded his support. "Talk to the men, Phil. Find out what happened. Determine if anyone had a grudge against Taylor."

Phil tensed. "Morale is good in the unit, sir. We haven't had any problems."

"That's how it seemed prior to this mission." The commander patted Phil's back. "But now everything has changed."

A fact Phil realized all too well. His focus for his entire career had been on doing what was right. His men called him a hard taskmaster, but he allowed no one to deviate from the rules he put in place—rules to ensure the safety of his men and the successful execution of each mission.

His decision to run an inherently dangerous live-fire exercise after putting his men through four strenuous days of intense, round-the-clock tactical training in the field would come under scrutiny. Fatigue led to mistakes, which is what some people would assume played into today's horrific accident.

Had there been a safety breakdown today? Phil had controlled the advancement and was responsible for everything that happened to his men on the simulated battlefield. Could he have inadvertently put Corporal Taylor in the line of fire?

He had been over the operations order that outlined the battle plan numerous times before the live-fire exercise. Tonight, he would retrace what he had done to ensure the checkpoints and phase lines and boundaries were correct.

That attention to detail had served him well and served the unit under his command well. But as quickly as a round exploded from the barrel of a gun, everything had changed today. Just as Lieutenant Colonel Knowlton had so pointedly mentioned.

"The Safety Officer has made a recommendation that an investigation be initiated," the battalion commander said. "The CID will begin their investigation tonight."

"Yes, sir."

Working hand in hand with the military police on post, the Criminal Investigation Division handled all major incidents and crimes that involved the military. Because a soldier had died, it was a given that the CID would be called onboard.

"We'll let the CID help us determine what happened," Knowlton said.

"Yes, sir." Phil saluted his battalion commander's retreating figure, then raised his hand to his forehead a second time in response to his first sergeant's salute.

Of medium build and pushing forty, First Sergeant Jerry Meyers' face wore a perpetual frown that seemed appropriate at the moment. He lowered his voice so only Phil could hear. "An agent from the Criminal Investigation Division is on the way, sir."

"Have the platoon leaders bring their men into formation on the edge of the range. No one leaves until I give the order."

The sergeant nodded. "Yes, sir."

"Taylor was part of First Platoon. Tell Lieutenant Bellows to keep his platoon separated from the rest of the company until I personally talk to the men."

"I'll pass that on to Lieutenant Bellows and notify the other platoon leaders to gather their men, as well." With a quick salute, the first sergeant double-timed to the far side of the range.

Footsteps sounded to Phil's left. He turned and spotted Jamison Steele walking purposefully toward him with an officer and enlisted man in tow. Phil had run into the CID agent at the Fort Rickman Club on more than one occasion and was impressed with his levelheaded attention to duty. If Jamison had been assigned to investigate the training incident, Phil could breathe a sigh of relief.

After a perfunctory greeting, Jamison introduced Major Bret Hansen, the medical examiner and pathologist at the hospital on post. The two men shook hands before the ME donned latex gloves and stooped to examine the body. Jamison also introduced Corporal Raynard Otis, who strung crime-scene tape around the area where the body lay and began to search the ground for evidence.

As the two men worked, Phil turned to the CID agent. "You've been assigned the case?"

"Negative. I'm here to secure the range and assist Major Hansen." Jamison looked over his shoulder toward the bleacher area. "Special Agent Kelly McQueen will be handling this one."

Phil's heart thumped against his chest as he followed Jamison's gaze and recognized the very determined complication walking toward them. More than anything, Phil didn't want his focus swayed off course by the pretty face that seemed to pop up everywhere he went on post.

Phil had heard some of the single officers grouse about the attractive CID agent. Her good looks weren't the problem. It was her no-nonsense attitude. A number of guys called her the Ice McQueen. And the fact that she'd won the Outstanding Marksmanship Award was off-putting to some.

Easy enough to understand their frustration. Kelly was an anomaly. Beautiful yet aloof, and 100 percent focused on her job. Phil had to admit he admired her for maintaining her distance from many of the men on post whose interests revolved around her pretty face instead of the strength of character she undoubtedly possessed.

He also understood her desire to keep her personal relationships separate from her military career. He had vowed long ago to never get involved with female personnel. When and if he settled down, it would be with a woman who wanted to be a stay-at-home mom with a houseful of children to love. Somehow that didn't go hand in hand with a career military gal who needed to be at Uncle Sam's beck and call.

Kelly McQueen might be good at what she did, but Phil had to keep his focus on the investigation and not the special agent. He didn't want sparks of interest to interfere with the work ahead. Instead, he wanted an answer to the question that pinged through his brain. How had one of his men shot and killed another soldier in the unit?

Biting down on his lip, he steeled himself to the ironic twist of events. Phil didn't need the Ice McQueen in his life. No matter how attracted he was to her.

Kelly hadn't expected Captain Thibodeaux's eyes to be as black as the night that had settled over the range. Nor had she expected the frown that furrowed his brow and tugged at his full lips. The guy had "Keep Out of My Business" written all over him. Even his hands were fisted, as if she were an adversary instead of someone assigned to help him get to the bottom of a very bad situation.

"Evening, Captain." She held out her CID identification. "I'm Special Agent Kelly McQueen with the Criminal Investigation Division on post."

"Phil Thibodeaux." He breathed in a lungful of air. "I'm aware of who you are, Agent McQueen."

"It's Kelly, please. We'll be working together to find out what happened today. I suggest we drop formalities."

"Yes, ma'am."

"I'd like to talk to the soldiers in your unit and determine if anyone saw anything outside the norm."

He raised his brow. "You mean like one of my men being shot?"

The Cajun may have dropped his accent but not his attitude. "That *is* why I'm here, Captain."

Before he could reply, she turned her gaze toward the ridgeline where Taylor's squad had made their final attack on foot. "Which of your platoons was advancing in this area?"

His brow furrowed. "Weren't you at the live-fire demonstration, ma'am?"

"That's correct, Captain, but my attention was on the visitors I was assigned to safeguard."

He hesitated for a moment before his shoulders relaxed ever so slightly and his hard-core expression softened.

Noting the visible signs of his change of attitude, Kelly regretted her own stubborn desire to always be on the offensive.

"Never let down your guard" had become a personal mantra. Her mother, when she had been alive, had pointed out numerous time that the tough facade Kelly tried to project was both a blessing and a curse.

Growing up as a headstrong teen, Kelly hadn't wanted advice from a woman who was a pushover when it came to Kelly's "here today, gone tomorrow" father. A little backbone and a firm no-you-can't-come-back attitude from her mother would have made life a lot more bearable for her only child. Not that Kelly was complaining. She had survived, thanks to an army recruiter who pointed out the benefits of enlisting in the military.

But all that was in the past, and at the moment, Kelly needed to deal with Captain Thibodeaux. To his credit, the captain had just lost a man to friendly fire and was still able to function. Perhaps she should cut him a little slack. Her initial assessment had been biased, no doubt, by his Cajun roots.

"First Platoon was advancing up this small hill." Phil finally provided the information she had requested. "The three squads had dismounted. The men were gaining ground on the enemy."

He pointed to where the soldiers had made their advance. "Corporal Taylor was on the far end of the squad, moving forward. The bullet hit just below his protective vest."

Kelly focused on the range, mentally seeing the attack unfold. "The other soldiers in the platoon were to the victim's right?"

"That's correct. The men were in their squads and spread out in a V formation, moving forward."

"How far apart were they?"

Phil shrugged. "Roughly eight to ten meters."

"And the other two platoons?"

"Were positioned farther east."

"Too far away to have shot into the First Platoon?"

"It's unlikely."

"But could have happened?" she pressed.

He nodded, his lips tight. "Yes, but as I mentioned, highly unlikely."

"Which means the shooter is probably one of the men in First Platoon."

The captain bristled. "This was a training accident, Agent McQueen. The soldier who accidentally dislodged a bullet that hit Corporal Taylor is not a shooter."

"Yet one of the guns fired the deadly round."

"Accidentally."

She tilted her head. "Are you sure of that, Captain?"

"Ma'am, most of the men in this unit just returned from a year in combat. They are well trained and competent. I'd stake my life on any of them."

She glanced at the soldier on the ground. "Regrettably, Corporal Taylor can't say the same."

Once again, they seemed at have hit an impasse. Attempting to give them both space, she walked to where the medical examiner knelt over the body. Her heart went out to the corporal, who didn't deserve to have his life end on a dusty army range in South Georgia.

Jamison approached her. His voice was low when he spoke. "The doc will have the bullet for us after the autopsy tomorrow. I called our lab at Fort Gillam and told them we'd need ballistics run."

Kelly nodded her approval as Jamison continued. "Once the lab comes up with a match, we'll have the serial number of the weapon that fired the bullet and the name of the soldier to whom the rifle had been issued."

Just as Jamison had mentioned, the investigation should be fairly straightforward, but complications were a fact of life when a death was involved. Uncovering the real reason a soldier had died could turn into a lengthy process.

She watched Phil give orders to his executive officer and first sergeant about securing the weapons and locking them in the arms room. Up close and personal, the captain was even better-looking than Kelly had realized. The eyes clinched the deal, along with the dimples that must be killers when he smiled. Not that he was smiling this evening. His rugged face was lined with concern and an underpinning of grief.

No doubt he felt for the loss of his soldier's life, but he also had to know his own career was on the line. If the captain had made a mistake, he'd be disciplined as well as the shooter. Phil had a reputation for being the pretty boy on post with the ladies and the man most likely to be promoted above his peers. Maybe the poster boy of Fort Rickman knew his moment of glory was coming to an end.

"With some luck, we might have this investigation under wraps within a few days," Kelly told Jamison. Then she could say goodbye and good riddance to Captain Thibodeaux. Until then, she had to be careful.

She knew all too well that a handsome face could turn a girl's heart. Her mother had been a perfect example. At least Kelly had enough sense to stay away from guys who promised everything and gave nothing but heartache in return.

The memory of her Cajun dad bubbled up like rancid oil. Kelly wouldn't take pity on anyone, even a handsome captain who, at this particular moment, looked like he needed a friend.

TWO

Phil glanced at the clock on the wall as he entered his company headquarters. Eight o'clock. He and Agent McQueen had talked to the unit as a whole. Both of them had addressed the terrible tragedy and the need to find out what had happened. Phil had encouraged the men to confide in their platoon leaders, squad leaders and the battalion chaplain. Tomorrow they would spend one-on-one time with each man in hopes of learning more.

Kelly had been supportive through it all, which Phil appreciated. Maybe having her in charge of the investigation wouldn't be a complication after all.

The next priority was to notify Mrs. Taylor of her husband's death. The wives had been briefed before the company road-marched to the field four days ago about the time of the unit's return to post. None of the family members expected their soldiers to be released from duty for another two hours.

Still, Phil wanted the chaplain and Taylor's platoon leader on the road as fast as possible to notify the corporal's next of kin. Phil wanted to be there, as well.

Currently, the special agent was overseeing the turn-in of weapons in the arms rooms. The serial number on each rifle would be checked and double-checked. She had mentioned returning to CID headquarters once the firearms were under lock and key.

If he had noticed one thing about the special agent tonight, it was that she was thorough. Her attention to detail had given him confidence the investigation would be handled by the book.

Earlier he had feared Kelly might be a distraction, but she understood the work that needed to be done, for which he was grateful. Cute as she was, the woman seemed keenly aware of the SOP—standard operation procedure—for the company and in no way hampered Phil's leadership or got in the way of the men doing their jobs.

As far as he could tell, she realized everyone was stretched thin from the four-day field exercise prior to live fire, and although she hadn't verbalized her opinion, she must have known their fatigue could have played into the incident today.

The battalion chaplain was on his way over to the company. A new guy named Sanchez, who'd recently transferred into post.

Together, along with Lieutenant Carl Bellows, a slender twenty-three-year-old who was in charge of First Platoon, the three officers would break the news to Mrs. Taylor. Not something to look forward to doing tonight, or any night for that matter.

Letting out a deep breath, Phil stepped into the latrine and slapped cold water on his face. Tired eyes stared back at him from the mirror. What would he tell Mrs. Taylor about her husband's death? Hopefully, the chaplain would offer the comfort Phil didn't know if he could provide tonight. All he knew was that Taylor shouldn't have died.

As he stepped from the latrine, the first sergeant approached him. "Sir, Chaplain Roger Sanchez is waiting in your office."

The chaplain stood about five-ten, with a square face and stocky build, and had new-to-the-army written all over him. He held a Bible in his left hand and accepted Phil's handshake with his right.

"Chaplain, thanks for helping me out this evening."

"No problem, sir."

Phil almost smiled. "Is Fort Rickman your first assignment?"

Sanchez nodded. "After Chaplains School."

"Good to have you with us. First rule to remember, we're both captains. You only need to 'sir' someone who's above you in rank."

Sanchez shook his head at his own mistake. "Guess I wasn't thinking."

"Well, there's a lot to learn. Tonight you'll get some experience in notification of next of kin." Phil explained about Corporal Taylor's death and the necessity of informing the family members.

"Taylor and his wife, Lola, lived on a farm his mother owns. The senior Mrs. Taylor—" Phil opened a file on his desk "—Mildred Taylor, the mom, has medical problems, although I'm not sure about the exact nature of her condition. We'll probably learn more tonight."

Sanchez nodded and then eyed the framed unit citations and awards on the wall behind Phil's desk. "You commanded C Company in Afghanistan?"

"That's right. We got back three months ago."

The chaplain shook his head. "So there was a long separation for the family prior to Corporal Taylor's death."

Phil narrowed his eyes. "I didn't say tonight would be easy, Chaplain."

Sanchez held his gaze. "And I never expected it would be. Just to set the record straight, I didn't become a chaplain for the easy jobs."

With that one statement, Phil's opinion of the chaplain went up tenfold.

"Lieutenant Bellows, the platoon leader, will meet us outside. He'll drive his own vehicle."

Phil grabbed his hat and motioned the chaplain forward just as the door to his office opened and Kelly McQueen stepped inside like a whirlwind of fresh air and energy.

"I thought you'd be at CID headquarters by now," he said.

"I'm on my way." She glanced at Sanchez, then back at Phil. "You said you were going to notify the next of kin?"

"That's right." He introduced her to the chaplain. "Lieutenant Bellows is meeting us outside, and the three of us will drive to the farmhouse."

"First Sergeant Meyers gave me directions," Kelly said. "The Taylor home is about five miles farther out from where I live. I'll join you there."

"Ah—?" Phil hadn't expected Kelly to go with them. "Do you think that's wise?"

She stood up a little straighter. "Wise?"

"Meaning it's late. Both Mrs. Taylors—the wife and the mother—will need time to grieve. We could drive out there tomorrow. I'll probably need to talk to the widow again."

Kelly nodded. "Perfect. But I want to see her tonight, as well. I have to stop by CID Headquarters for a few minutes, but I'll meet you at the farmhouse."

She smiled at Sanchez. "Nice to meet you, Chaplain." Turning on her heel, she left the office and Phil to stare after her.

His phone rang. Lieutenant Bellows's voice sounded fatigued when he answered. "Sir, can you give me about fifteen minutes? Private Benjamin Stanley wants to talk to me about what happened today."

"He's one of our new recruits."

"Yes, sir. Seems he's pretty shook up."

Phil glanced at his watch. "Get here as soon as you can."

The lieutenant drove up in front of the company head-quarters just as Phil and the chaplain left the building fifteen minutes later. After introducing the two men, Lieutenant Bellows shared his own concern for the private.

"Stanley's young and impressionable. From what he said, this is the first time he's seen someone die. I've got Staff Sergeant Gates with him now."

Phil turned to the chaplain. "Gates is one of Lieutenant Bellow's squad leaders. He's mid-thirties and fairly squared away. If he can't reassure Stanley, I may ask you to talk to him tomorrow. He's a good kid who loves the Lord and knows his Bible, but he's still got a lot to learn."

The chaplain smiled. "I can relate to that. I'd be happy to pray with him. Inviting God into any situation usually brings comfort to those experiencing difficulty."

Although Phil didn't personally agree with the chaplain, he knew Stanley would benefit from the outreach.

Phil turned to the lieutenant. "Let me know what Gates has to say. If Stanley's still upset, we can call the chaplain in the morning."

"Yes, sir. Some of the other men have been talking about Corporal Taylor. Evidently things hadn't been too good on the home front since the company redeployed back to the States. Sounds like he and his wife were having problems."

"At Chaplains School, we talked about how marital problems escalate once the soldiers redeploy home," Sanchez said.

Phil nodded. "Unfortunately the separations are hard on family members as well as the soldiers."

"Which will probably compound the grieving process for Mrs. Taylor."

The chaplain was right. Phil kept thinking about Taylor and his wife as he and Sanchez headed to the parking lot.

Phil had instructed Bellows to drive ahead and wait for him at the farm, assuring the lieutenant they wouldn't be far behind him.

Once on the way, Phil made a quick detour that took them past the CID headquarters. He scanned the parking lot, hoping to spot Kelly in case she wanted to follow them, but her Toyota Corolla wasn't in sight.

Maybe she had another stop to make. No reason for Phil to be concerned. Sergeant Meyers had given her directions, and she said she would meet them at the Taylor home. From everything he had seen tonight, Kelly could take care of herself.

As difficult as the notification would be, Phil's mood lifted ever so slightly when he thought of seeing her again. Then he clamped down on his jaw. What was wrong with him? The last person he should be thinking about was the CID agent. Yet, for some reason, Kelly McQueen was the only thing his mind wanted to focus on tonight.

The sun had set hours ago, and darkness, thick as tar, enveloped South Georgia as Kelly left Fort Rickman and headed north along the two-lane road that led through Freemont and past the nursing home where her mother had lived for the last year of her life.

A lump filled Kelly's throat at the memory of sitting at her dying mother's bedside. Coronary obstructive pulmonary disease had sapped her energy and left her gasping for air. In spite of the oxygen concentrator that had become her constant companion, her mother's body had weakened until death seemed almost a welcome alternative to the fragile existence that had held her bound between this world and the next.

Just a short distance beyond the nursing facility, Kelly spied her own home, which sat back from the road. Never expecting to be tied up for so long on post, Kelly had failed to leave a light on when she left the house earlier today. Now the brick ranch looked dark and foreboding and recessed with shadows from the sliver of moon that hung low in the sky.

Passing her house, she sped north along the Freemont Road and into a stretch of no-man's-land flanked by a thick forest of trees on each side of the asphalt. Kelly turned her lights to high beam and flicked her gaze over not only the pavement but also the shoulder and the edge of the forest.

Deer often darted out from the underbrush, causing accidents and injuries to both car and driver. The only motion she saw came from the branches that swayed in the wind and the flutter of leaves that fell one after another from the canopy of boughs overhead.

She checked her odometer. Five miles into the darkness seemed an eternity tonight. Maybe it was the anticipation of knowing the captain was already at the farmhouse. She wanted to be on the scene when he and the chaplain broke the news to Corporal Taylor's widow. The initial reactions from loved ones could be telling, especially in a criminal investigation.

At this point, Kelly had no evidence to indicate foul play. A training accident more than likely would be the final determination. Tomorrow she would review Phil's operations order to determine if there were any safety issues with the plan.

Phil Thibodeaux seemed competent and concerned about his soldiers. Hard to imagine he had made a blatant mistake, but the unit had been in the field for the past four days, and fatigue could be a significant factor. As much as Phil seemed to have his act together, looks could be deceiving.

Her father's face floated through her mind. Everything about that no-good Cajun had been a sham. Each time he had returned home, he had taken her mother for a ride, wiping out her money and her emotional stability. When he tired of pretending to love her, he hightailed it out of Savannah and headed west, more often than not back to his beloved bayou.

Even as a child, Kelly had questioned her father's here-again gone-again behavior. By puberty, she recognized him for who he really was—a conniver who thought only of himself. She'd asked God to take him out of her life, but God seemed occupied with other people's problems instead of hers. When her dad had become abusive to her mother, she'd prayed he would be attacked by snakes and eaten by alligators in the Louisiana swamps he loved more than his own daughter.

God hadn't answered that prayer, either.

Eventually she decided that since she couldn't count on her earthly father, she shouldn't rely on her heavenly one, either. Instead she vowed to never be subservient to a man, like her mother had been whenever her father came back to Savannah with his proverbial hat in hand and a string of excuses for being gone so long.

Kelly shoved her hair away from her face. Luckily she had moved beyond the pain of growing up in a dysfunctional family and being the only one to have at least a smattering of common sense, which she needed to use today instead of returning to memories that should remain buried under a thick layer of Mississippi Delta mud.

She glanced once again at the odometer. Another mile until she would reach the turnoff for the farm, if the first sergeant's directions were accurate. Just in case he had guesstimated the mileage, she watched for a mailbox at the roadside along with a split rail fence, which supposedly were the only landmarks that identified the long driveway that led to the Taylor home.

Up ahead, the road curved to the right. Kelly eased her

foot off the gas. Halfway into the turn, a teenager dashed out from nowhere and ran across the road. For a second, he was spotlighted in the beam of her headlights.

Shaved head, tattoos, body piercings and blood.

Her heart jolted.

Kelly stomped on the brakes and gripped the steering wheel as the tires skidded over the pavement, narrowly missing the boy.

In the blink of an eye, he was gone.

Adrenaline coursed through her veins and rammed her pulse into high gear. Gasping at the close call, she steered the car to the edge of the road and leaned back against the headrest. A roar of disbelief filled her ears at what had almost happened.

Kyle Foglio?

The teen had visited his lieutenant colonel father on post more than two years ago when Kelly had first hauled him in for questioning. Kyle had turned explosive, and the father had sent him back to be with his first wife, the boy's mother, who lived up north. On one other occasion Kelly had run into the teen on Fort Rickman property, but that, too, hadn't ended well.

Doing an instant rewind of the near miss, Kelly watched in her mind's eye as Kyle raised his right hand to his face to block the glare of the headlights. Easy enough to recognize the tattoos and body metal. She had seen him in the bleachers today at the live-fire demonstration, sitting next to a teenage girl, so she had known he was in the area. The kid could be trouble, and Kelly had made sure on his previous two visits that he toed a straight line while he was on post. Not that Kyle had appreciated her intervention.

What she hadn't expected tonight were the cuts that slashed through the underside of his forearms and the blood that had spattered his shirt. How had he been injured, and why had he run into the underbrush?

Reaching under her seat, Kelly grabbed her Maglite and stepped onto the pavement. The temperature had dropped, and she pulled her navy-blue windbreaker closed and shined the light over the roadway, picking out the droplets of blood that had splattered across the asphalt. The kid should be at the emergency room getting medical treatment instead of running through the woods.

"Kyle?" She shined the light into the woods. An eerie sense of foreboding tingled along her spine. "I want to help you, Kyle."

Hearing no response, she followed the trail of blood. The smell of Georgia clay and rotting leaves rose from the dew-dampened earth. She pushed into the dense forest where prickly thorns scraped against her hand as she shoved her way deeper into the darkness.

"Kyle?"

Even the cicadas and tree frogs were silent tonight.

She aimed the Maglite into the underbrush. The beam flickered. Giving the flashlight a firm shake, she was rewarded with the return of a powerful beam that eventually revealed a dirt path and a clearing beyond.

Kelly headed for the open space. Her foot stepped onto a bed of fallen leaves. Something wrapped around her ankle. Her heart pounded an instant warning.

Before she could glance down, a whoosh of air and a powerful jerk knocked the flashlight from her hand and propelled her airborne in a topsy-turvy swirl of motion.

A gasp escaped her lips, and her stomach roiled in protest. The forest twirled around her. Heart pounding in her throat, she saw the earth below and realized she was dangling upside down. Her leg burned with pain from the jolt and the rope that tightened around her ankle. What had she gotten tangled up in? Some type of animal trap?

Blood rushed to her head. She tried to reach up and grab the thick hemp that held her bound. When that failed, she grasped her holster and unsheathed her weapon. Her fingers latched onto the cold steel. The only way to get down was to shoot the rope in two.

The sound of twigs breaking and the crackle of leaves came from the dense underbrush. A small animal was skittering for shelter or—?

Footsteps.

Her already erratic heartbeat cranked up a notch.

Friend or foe?

On the ground far below where she had dropped it, the flashlight dimmed and the beam faded into darkness. Her pulse hammered in her ears.

She gripped the gun, her finger firm against the trigger. Was Kyle coming back for her or was someone else roaming through the forest? And if so, why?

Surely Phil would still be talking to the two Mrs. Taylors. Hopefully, he'd see her car when he left the farmhouse and headed back to town, but no telling how soon that would be.

She listened for the sound of a car engine, hearing nothing except the silent forest that seemed to close in around her. The stillness was more frightening than the rustling had been moments earlier. Where was he...or it?

Something slithered through the dried leaves. Her gut tightened with revulsion. She hated snakes.

Another twig snapped. Something larger than a snake was headed her way.

She shivered as a cold chill wrapped her in fear thick enough to taste. Holding the gun, she tried to steady her aim.

Branches parted. In the darkness, she couldn't identify much more than a huge bulk that stepped toward the clearing.

Never let them know you're afraid. The thought rattled through her mind. She mustered her courage, raised her gun and took aim.

THREE

"What are you doing in that tree, Kelly?"

"Phil?"

His eyes had adjusted to the darkness, and even from this distance, he could make out her slender body as well as the barrel of the Sig Sauer aimed directly at him.

"Don't just stand there. Get me down." She sounded piqued.

"No, ma'am. Not until you holster your weapon."

"What?"

"The gun, Kelly. I don't trust anyone who's pointing a nine-millimeter at my midsection."

She harrumphed. "I wasn't planning to shoot you. I heard a noise and thought—"

The words stuck in her throat, but she complied with his request and returned the weapon to her hip holster.

Phil reached for her just as he had wanted to do the moment he had stepped into the clearing and had seen she was in trouble. "Wrap your arms around my neck."

She complied without an outburst, for which he was grateful. Her leg had to hurt, and her skin felt cold and clammy. He wouldn't mention shock, but that was a concern. The dropping temperature and her lightweight jacket didn't help.

Pulling a knife from his pocket, he sawed through the rope

and gently lowered her feet to the ground while his arms remained clasped around her waist. She felt soft and fragile and…well, like a woman.

His own pulse raced as he held her tight against his chest, trying to transmit the heat from his body back into hers. She closed her eyes, and a thread of worry coursed along his spine. "Kelly?"

Her breath fanned his flesh and wreaked havoc with his nerve endings. "Kelly? Answer me."

Thankfully, her eyes blinked open, but she appeared dazed. Then, before he could say anything to reassure her, she pushed her hands against his chest with such force that he took a step back to balance the shift in weight.

Her erratic behavior sent up a warning flag. "You blacked out."

She put her hands on her hips and rolled her eyes. "You saw me hanging upside down, Phil. Did I look unconscious?"

Relieved by her outburst, he almost laughed. "Next time remind me to leave you in the tree."

"Right."

Hearing a hint of levity mixed with her frustration, he pulled his cell phone from his pocket and hit speed dial. "Chaplain Sanchez, this is Captain Thibodeaux. I found Agent McQueen. We'll meet you back at her car."

Phil flipped his cell closed and stared down at Kelly. Her blond hair was disheveled, but she was trying to maintain some semblance of composure.

"The chaplain checked the other side of the roadway while I headed this direction," Phil said. "Now tell me what you were doing out here."

She quickly explained about almost running into the teenager. "He was sitting in the bleachers with a teenage girl at the live-fire exercise today and looked like he might have cleaned up his image a bit. But tonight there was blood on his shirt, and the inside of his arms appeared to have been cut."

Phil's eyes searched the darkness in case the injured teen was still around. "Did he recognize you?"

"Probably not with the glare of the headlights. After the near miss, he had to be as shook up as I was." She glanced down at her Maglite. "If you've got a flashlight or extra batteries for mine, we can search the area."

She took a step to retrieve the light and almost fell.

He grabbed her elbow to steady her. "Hold up a minute."

Kelly pulled her arm out of his grasp. "I'm fine, Phil."

But he knew she wasn't. He looked down and saw the determination she tried to hold in place. "We'll search the area in daylight, Kelly. Right now you need to get off that leg."

She took another step, only to stumble again. "It's a pulled muscle, nothing more."

Phil had had enough of her attempt to walk. He leaned over and grabbed her flashlight, then, before she could object, he lifted her into his arms.

"Put me down." She struggled to free herself.

"I will when we get to your car. Right now, save both of us some energy and cooperate."

She let out an exasperated breath and thankfully didn't utter another word until he stepped onto the pavement.

"I can walk across the street by myself." She wiggled to free herself from his hold.

"Humor me, Agent McQueen."

"It's Kelly."

"Okay. Humor me, Kelly."

Sanchez stood by her car. He opened the passenger door and stepped aside as Phil placed her carefully on the front seat.

Kelly's brow wrinkled. "I thought both of you were already at the farmhouse."

"We got hung up on post. Lieutenant Bellows went on ahead of us. He's probably waiting at the turnoff to the farm." Phil bent to examine her leg.

She tried to swat his hands away. "That's not necessary."

He sat back on his haunches and stared at her. "Here's the deal. Either I examine your ankle now or I drive you back to the emergency room on post and have the doctor on duty take a look at you."

She raised her chin and closed her eyes for a long moment. When she opened them, she nodded. "All right. Check my leg. Then I'm going with you to the farmhouse."

"If your leg's not broken," he said.

"It's merely a sprain."

Phil worked his fingers over her narrow ankle until his thumb gently pressed a tender spot. She jerked.

"Chaplain, there's a first aid kit in the back of my pickup. Would you get it for me?"

Once Sanchez handed the kit to Phil, he pulled out an ACE bandage and wrapped it snugly around her ankle. "That should help. At least until I can get you home."

"You have to talk to Mrs. Taylor, and I'm going with you."

The woman could be stubborn, but he knew better than to voice that observation. Instead he remained quiet as he handed the first aid kit back to Sanchez. "I'll drive Agent McQueen's vehicle. You follow in my truck."

Once Phil slipped behind the wheel, he glanced at her and then in the rearview mirror to ensure the chaplain was ready before he started the engine. "We'll pay Mrs. Taylor a visit and tell her about her husband. When we return tomorrow, we'll ask her why a series of traps was rigged on the land not far from her mother-in-law's property line."

Kelly's eyes widened. "You saw more than one?"

"As dark as it was, I can't be sure, but I thought I passed a couple of rigged snares on my way to find you."

"Animal traps?"

Phil shrugged. "Could be, but if so, they were looking for mighty big critters. Any bear sightings in the area?"

"I haven't heard of any."

"Tigers or lions?"

He could see a hint of a smile tug at her sweet lips. "Not recently."

"Then as near as I can determine, the traps were set to catch another type of game."

Kelly's smile faded. "You mean the human kind."

"Roger that." Phil steered the car onto the road. "Wonder what's going on in these woods that someone wants to keep off-limits?"

"And why," Kelly added, "was a teenage boy, who was at a live-fire demonstration on post earlier today, wandering around in the night?"

Kelly's leg hurt. Not that she would mention her discomfort to Phil. The mishap in the woods had caused him too much of a delay already. He and the chaplain needed to notify Taylor's widow of what had happened as soon as possible. A difficult task, to say the least.

Still concerned about the wounded teen, Kelly called the Freemont police and told the dispatcher about the injured youth. He promised to send an officer to check the woods in case Kyle was still in the area.

"I'll call them back tomorrow and see if they found Kyle," Kelly said once she hung up.

Phil nodded, then pulled his eyes from the road and glanced at her injured leg. "How are you doing?"

"Fine."

"Really?"

"It smarts a bit, but nothing I can't handle."

"I still think you need to have it X-rayed."

"A couple doses of ibuprofen and I'll be good as new."

"Right."

As they rounded a bend in the road, Kelly spied the mailbox and the split rail fence. Phil pulled up next to another car that had stopped just before the narrow dirt driveway.

Lieutenant Bellows lowered his window. "I was beginning to get worried, sir, when you didn't show up. Everything okay?"

"We had a slight delay. Is this the place?"

"Yes, sir. As I mentioned, Corporal Taylor and his wife lived with his mom."

Phil glanced at the farmhouse sitting on a knoll in the distance. "Let's get this done."

"Yes, sir."

The three vehicles turned onto the drive and headed along a path marked with potholes to a gravel-covered parking area to the left of the house. A porch light illuminated the clearing, sending long shadows into the darkness.

"Stay put and I'll come around the car to help you," Phil said to Kelly as he opened his own door. Before he could reach the passenger side, she had stepped onto the gravel.

Putting weight on her ankle sent a razor-sharp pain straight up her leg. She groaned. Not loud, but loud enough for him to extend his arm and grab her elbow.

"I said I'd help you." He closed her door.

She was grateful the darkness hid her flushed cheeks. She didn't need the handsome captain, who was standing way too close, to realize she was anything but composed at the present moment.

"I'm fine, really." She tried to extricate her arm from his hold, but he continued to support her.

"The gravel is uneven, Kelly."

She shoved her chin up a notch and averted his gaze. Her body's reaction to his nearness must be the result of the upside-down tumble she'd had in the woods. Everything inside her was out of kilter, including her ability to remain focused on anything except the tall, broad-shouldered guy who had become her shadow.

Surely he was aware of the effect he had on women. Kelly had seen him numerous times at the club on post surrounded by a gaggle of beautiful women. Okay, maybe that was stretching the point. After all, she wasn't even sure how many women constituted a gaggle. Three? Four? Maybe five?

But the women she *had* seen fawning over Phil had been tall and svelte and drop-dead gorgeous. Thinking of her own petite frame, Kelly knew she was anything but svelte. Slender, maybe. Intelligent, yes. But svelte? Definitely not!

Squaring her shoulders, she limped toward the porch and grasped the railing as she climbed the stairs with Phil at her side, his hand supporting her. He leaned closer to ensure she could navigate the last step, causing her knees to almost buckle. Seemed the attentive captain had a strange effect on her equilibrium.

At least she remained upright thanks to his hold on her arm, which proved the captain *was* good for something. Instantly, she regretted the internal sarcasm.

"You're too critical of men." Her mother's words came back to taunt her. Kelly didn't need the mental recollection of a chastisement she had heard too often growing up, which was usually followed by, "Your father loves you in his own way."

Her mother painted a picture of their little family that was anything but pretty to Kelly. Invariably, she chose to ignore the very obvious fact that Kelly's father had never seen the need to marry her mother.

Kelly was a McQueen—her mother's maiden name—instead of a LeBlanc. In Kelly's opinion, the lack of a marriage certificate proved her father, Charles LeBlanc, was only interested in sweet-talking her mother and not establishing a long-term relationship with either her mother or his only child.

Daddy dearest had died thirteen years ago on a dismal night she tried to block out of her mind. Not that she was always successful.

Still holding her elbow, Phil raised his hand to knock just as the farmhouse door flew open. A woman with chestnut hair stood in the doorway, her green eyes alight with expectation. Confusion quickly took the place of the initial glimmer of hope. Her forehead wrinkled and her hand flew to her heart.

"It's Rick, isn't it? What happened?"

"I'm Captain Thibodeaux, ma'am. Commander of C Company. We met at the family picnic shortly after the unit returned from Afghanistan."

Mrs. Taylor nodded.

He pointed to the others. "Special Agent Kelly McQueen from the CID office, Chaplain Sanchez and Lieutenant Bellows. May we come in?"

Phil removed his hat as he opened the screen door, motioned Kelly inside and then followed her into the living area along with the chaplain and lieutenant.

The wife turned to stare at them, her eyes wide with worry. "Where's Rick?"

Phil's face wore the grief they all were feeling. "Ma'am, I'm sorry. There was an accident. Your husband was hit by a live round."

"Oh, dear God, no." She slumped onto the couch. The chaplain hastened to her side. "Was…was anyone else hurt?" she asked.

"Only Corporal Taylor, ma'am." Phil pulled in a deep breath. "The medics were on-site. They tried their best, but your husband suffered a massive loss of blood and couldn't be saved."

She lowered her face into her hands and moaned. "Why?" she repeated over and over again. The lieutenant huddled over her.

Kelly watched as the men offered words of comfort. Mrs. Taylor shook her head back and forth and began to cry. Her heart-wrenching sobs soon filled the small living area. The chaplain handed her his handkerchief, which she accepted, but her face remained buried in her hands.

Mrs. Taylor appeared to be in her mid-thirties, which was at least half a decade older than her deceased husband. Medium height and slight of build, she had appeared capable and in control when she'd first opened the door. Kelly's initial impression was of a strong woman who usually got what she wanted.

Now, sympathy for the grieving widow welled up within Kelly, overriding her attempt to look at the situation with an impartial eye. A lump lodged in her throat and sorrow wrapped her in a tight hold. No matter how competent Mrs. Taylor seemed, nor how much any one of them regretted what had happened just a short time ago, Kelly couldn't do anything to change today's tragic events.

Wrapping her arms around her waist, she stepped into the hallway, partly in hopes of distancing herself from the pitiful site of the broken widow and partly because she was aware of another sound.

Above Mrs. Taylor's sobs, Kelly heard a feeble call for help. The men, hovering around the grieving widow, seemed oblivious to the frail voice that cried out once again.

She followed the cries to a small bedroom at the rear of the house. The door hung ajar. Peering into the darkened interior, she saw a hospital bed with the side rails raised.

Kelly stepped toward the pile of covers that nearly hid the

wrinkled prune of a face that stared up at her. Big eyes—as blue as the sky on a summer's day—blinked open.

"Mrs. Taylor." Before Kelly could say anything else the sound of clipped heels signaled someone's annoyance and approach. Kelly turned to find Lola Taylor standing in the doorway.

"I glanced up as you left the living room." The widow's face was blotched from crying, but her eyes reflected anger instead of sorrow. "What are you doing in here?"

"I heard someone call for help," Kelly quickly explained.

"My mother-in-law suffers from dementia. She doesn't understand what's going on. You didn't mention—"

Kelly shook her head. "I haven't said anything."

The younger Mrs. Taylor swiped her hand over her cheeks to wipe away her tears before she approached the bed and smiled down at her mother-in-law. The senior Mrs. Taylor focused her gaze on Kelly. Her frail lips moved as if she was trying to speak.

"Mildred, it's time for your medicine." Lola grabbed a bottle on the side table, an extra-strength analgesic sold over the counter. She spilled two pills into her hand and reached for a glass of water on the nightstand.

"Let me help." Kelly raised the older woman's shoulders off the pillow so she could swallow the pills. Mildred's gray hair was pulled back from her face and appeared freshly combed, but an odor of urine wafted up from the crumpled bedding.

Once she had taken the pills, Kelly gently lowered her head back to the pillow and pulled the covers up around the woman's shoulders, feeling a stab of guilt at her own inability to have cared for her mother at home.

Being in the military meant Kelly could be sent anywhere on a moment's notice. She had needed a stable environment for her mother, and the local nursing home had been the best option at the time.

Plus, keeping her mom in her own home would have meant round-the-clock care, which wasn't possible on their limited incomes. Her mother had nothing more than a small social security check coming in each month, and Kelly's warrant officer pay had been stretched thin just to cover the few extras her mother needed.

Mildred's eyes drooped closed, and Kelly turned from the bed. As she did, her gaze took in the wide assortment of sleeping pills and over-the-counter pain medications on the nightstand.

Phil appeared in the doorway. "Everything okay?"

Kelly nodded. "I heard a call for help and found Corporal Taylor's mother."

He glanced at the now-sleeping woman and then at the widow before he lifted his brow to Kelly. She nodded, hoping he would pick up on her nonverbal cue that she would explain what had happened once they had left the house.

Turning to the widow, Kelly asked, "Do you have relatives in the area?"

Lola shook her head. "My family is from Kentucky, and Rick was an only child. But I have friends in town."

"How long have you lived here?"

"A little over a year. Rick and I were married fourteen months ago. He was stationed at Fort Knox when we met and was on orders for Fort Rickman. We moved to Freemont a month before he deployed to Afghanistan."

"You were practically newlyweds." As soon as the words left Kelly's mouth, she wanted to reel them in again.

Lola's face clouded. "Rick said military life would be an adventure. I never thought it would end like this."

Kelly's heart went out to the widow. She opened her arms and pulled her close, feeling her slender frame shake with grief. Kelly patted her back and tried to think of something to say to lessen the load this woman carried. Nothing came to mind except that life is fragile, which someone had mentioned at her own mother's funeral. The memory caused Kelly's eyes to burn. Phil stood in the doorway, his gaze lowered, his face drawn.

For a long moment, the only sounds in the room were the heavy pull of the old woman's breathing and Lola's sobs. Eventually, she stopped crying and turned away from Kelly to grab a handful of tissues from a box on the bedside table. She dabbed at her eyes, and when she glanced back at Kelly, her face was surprisingly clear and she appeared in control once again.

"It's been a long day," she admitted, motioning them into the hallway.

"A survival assistance officer will be assigned to help you with all the death notifications and paperwork," Phil said as they walked back to the living room.

"My husband's insurance?"

"Yes, ma'am. He'll guide you in completing the necessary forms so you can receive the money as soon as possible. The company and the entire battalion stand ready to assist you. You have Lieutenant Bellows's phone number at the platoon?"

She nodded.

Phil handed her his own card. "Don't hesitate to call the company if you can't reach Lieutenant Bellows. Perhaps tomorrow we can return to discuss any arrangements you would like to have for your husband's interment."

"Tomorrow?" She seemed unsure.

"Someone will phone you first."

"Yes, of course."

Lieutenant Bellows stood. "Mrs. Taylor, is there anyone who can stay with you tonight? Perhaps a friend?"

She stepped toward the door as if ready for them to leave. "I'll be all right."

"Are you sure you feel like being alone, ma'am?" Phil asked.

She nodded. "I'm not alone, Captain. My mother-in-law is with me. We'll be fine. Her mind is sometimes more clear in the morning. I'll tell her about Rick's death after her breakfast tomorrow."

As much as Kelly hated to leave the widow, she knew Lola wanted and perhaps needed her privacy now. Phil would call her in the morning and make arrangements for them to visit again. Once a survivor assistance officer was selected, that person would be her connection to the military and a support throughout the next few months as Mrs. Taylor tried to get her life in order.

Kelly held out her hand. "Mrs. Taylor, I'd like to talk to you tomorrow. I'll come out with Captain Thibodeaux."

Her eyes narrowed as she glanced from the CID agent to Phil. "What do you need to discuss?"

"I'm investigating your husband's death. I'd like to hear more about what his interests were outside of the military. Perhaps something pertaining to his off-duty time could have had bearing on what happened this evening."

The widow shook her head. "I don't see how that could be."

Before Kelly could answer, Phil tapped her shoulder and nodded toward the door. "I'll call you tomorrow," he said to Mrs. Taylor.

The cool night air swirled around the small military entourage as they stepped onto the porch. The door closed behind them. Phil supported Kelly as she hobbled down the stairs.

A stiff breeze picked at her jacket. She pulled the edges

closed. Patting the slick waterproof fabric, she expected to feel moisture from Lola's tears. Instead, the fabric was dry.

Turning to look over her shoulder at the farmhouse, Kelly spotted a curtain pulled back ever so slightly in the living room window.

A second gust of wind assaulted her. Kelly shivered.

Phil protectively placed his hand on her shoulder. "Cold?"

She shook her head and stepped toward the car door he held open. "Confused is more like it."

"Probably that mishap you had earlier," he said.

She would let him think what he wanted, but being caught in a snare wasn't the reason for the way she felt. The real problem was trying to sort through a number of mismatched signals from the widow. The woman had sobbed in Kelly's arm without producing tears to wet her jacket. But something else didn't add up in the CID agent's mind.

If Mildred Taylor was as sickly as she appeared, surely she would be under medical care, yet all of the bottles on the nightstand were over-the-counter painkillers and sleeping pills. Strange that none of her medication had been prescribed by a doctor.

FOUR

"I'll drive Special Agent McQueen home, if you both follow me," Phil said to Bellows and the chaplain after he had closed the passenger door and rounded the car to the driver's side. "Carl, can you give the chaplain a lift back to the company?"

The lieutenant nodded. "No problem, sir."

The chaplain and platoon leader headed for the other two parked vehicles while Phil slipped behind the wheel of Kelly's car.

"I can drive myself home," she insisted.

He smiled at her continual attempt to be in control of every situation. "You probably could. But since your right leg is injured, why don't you accept my help? That way I won't have to worry about you."

She returned his smile, which he took as a good sign. Maybe he was making headway with her. They needed to work together, and a little less go-it-alone determination on her part would make the job a whole lot easier.

He stuck the key in the ignition and started the engine, but his eyes were drawn to a light that flickered on in the senior Mrs. Taylor's bedroom at the rear of the house.

Kelly followed his gaze. "What's your take on Lola Taylor?"

He put the gear in Reverse. "Hard to say. She was all over

the map tonight, sobbing in the living room and then almost confrontational about her mother-in-law in the bedroom."

"My thoughts exactly, although we both know that grief can manifest in strange ways."

"That's true, yet—" he shrugged. "—something seemed off tonight. I didn't want to leave either woman alone, but I got the distinct impression Mrs. Lola Taylor felt we had overstayed our welcome."

After turning the car around, Phil headed along the driveway. At the gate he turned right, toward Freemont, with the chaplain and lieutenant following in the rear.

On each side of the road, tall pine trees mixed with hardwoods whose branches formed a canopy over the two lanes of asphalt. In the daytime, the thick forest of autumn foliage would be visible, but tonight the trees were cloaked in darkness. The headlights cut a path into the night, exposing patches of leaves that lay scattered across the roadway. With each gust of wind, more fell like confetti into the beam of the headlights.

The tires hummed over the roadway. Phil glanced at Kelly, who seemed lost in her own world. "Penny for your thoughts," he said.

She turned, seemingly embarrassed by her own reticence. "Sorry. Guess I'm not good company."

"There's nothing wrong with being quiet, but sometimes talking helps."

She nodded and raked her hand through her hair. "I was thinking about everything that happened today and how life can change in an instant."

"Usually not for the better."

She raised her brow. "Meaning?"

"Meaning good things take time to develop. Think about how long it takes to form a friendship or build on a relationship. When tragedy strikes it happens quickly, often in the blink of an eye. A heart attack. An auto accident. A misfire of a rifle."

"Is that what occurred today?"

He shook his head. "I don't know."

"Ballistics will identify the rifle. We could have answers within the next couple of days."

"I keep thinking about the men in my company. How many of them are lying on their bunks tonight, wondering if they could have shot the fatal round?"

"Sounds to me as if the company commander is concerned about his men. That's the mark of a good officer and a good commander."

Phil gazed at the road. "A commander ensures every precaution is taken to keep the men and women in his unit safe."

"Are you feeling guilty?"

"Not guilty, but responsible. My job is to train my men so they're combat ready and can accomplish the mission if they're called into battle."

"Accidents happen under the best or the worst of circumstances," she offered.

"Which doesn't justify what happened today."

"We'll know more tomorrow, Phil. Give it time. The questions troubling you tonight will be answered."

Once again, he focused on the road and tried to calm the inner turmoil he had felt ever since he had ordered the cease-fire. Maybe Kelly was right. He needed to give the investigation time. Hopefully, in a few days the truth would come to light.

They drove in silence until Kelly pointed to the brick ranch that sat back from the road. "That's my house on the left." Although bathed in darkness, the home and surrounding yard appeared neat and appealing.

Phil turned onto the drive and parked in front of the

garage. The chaplain pulled the pickup to a stop behind Kelly's car. Climbing out, he tossed the keys to Phil.

"I'll see you both in the morning." The chaplain waved, then crawled into the lieutenant's car, and the two men headed back to post.

Phil glanced down at the console. "I'll pull your car into the garage if you tell me where you hide the automatic opener."

"It's under the visor," Kelly said. "But just leave the car parked here. I can move it inside later."

He shook his head. "No way. You need to keep pressure off that leg of yours. Go into the house, and I'll bring the keys to you."

She stepped out of the car and then hesitated before closing the passenger door.

Noticing the strained look on her face, he backtracked. "I won't come in if you don't want me to."

She smiled. A good sign. "Actually, I was thinking you look tired, Phil. Would a cup of coffee help?"

He chuckled. "You must have read my mind."

"Hardly. But the bags under your eyes were a dead give-away. I bet you didn't sleep while you were in the field."

He shrugged. "You know how it is. Too many details to manage."

"Then I'll make the coffee extra strong," she said over her shoulder as she unlocked the front door and stepped inside.

Phil found the automatic opener and pushed the remote button, noting the meticulously clean garage as the heavy door rolled open. Not even a cobweb in the corner. Evidently, the CID agent didn't clutter up her garage with junk. He could probably say the same thing about her life.

Kelly was different from most of the women he knew, with their baubles and bracelets and big purses that held everything imaginable. In contrast, Kelly seemed neat and compact. Nothing extra, but all quality.

He rubbed his hand over his jaw and smiled as he climbed from the car. Actually, she was a refreshing change of pace. Eyeing the back entrance that led from the garage to the house, Phil opted to play it safe by knocking on the front door.

Kelly had been nice enough to invite him in for coffee. He wanted to mind his manners and not spook her into rescinding the invitation. Right now coffee was just what he needed.

"It's unlocked," she called in response to his knock.

Phil turned the knob and stepped into a small but inviting living room decorated in blue and green. A plaid couch and an overstuffed chair in a matching floral print were arranged around a glass-top coffee table that gave the place an open, airy feel.

Colorful watercolors of historic Savannah homes hung on the walls. He had visited the old part of the city a number of times when he'd been on temporary duty in nearby Fort Stewart.

A curio stand in the corner contained a collection of delicate teacups and matching saucers, along with pictures of a much younger Kelly and a woman she resembled. Probably her mom.

"I'm in the kitchen," Kelly called to him.

Phil followed the sound of her voice and the smell of fresh-ground coffee into a cozy kitchen decorated in shades of yellow. Standing at the counter, she turned to greet him. Her eyes twinkled as bright as the stars in the sky. Something had lifted from her shoulders—perhaps the stress of the day or the investigation—and for an instant, he wished he could come home with Kelly on a regular basis.

She had removed her jacket and her sidearm, which lay on

a buffet in the dining area. As he stepped closer, she poured water into the coffeepot.

"Can I help with something?" he asked.

"There's a pecan pie in the fridge. Pull it out, if you're hungry."

"You bake?"

She rolled her eyes. "What? Doesn't go with the CID role?"

He laughed as he removed the heavy ceramic pie plate from the cool refrigerator. The rich topping of pecans and the flaky fluted crust made his mouth water. "I'm not complaining. Pecan pie's a favorite of mine."

Her expression warmed. "Mine, too. And something every girl from Savannah knows how to bake."

"Paula Deen, right?"

"Ah, excuse me." She playfully huffed. "This recipe comes from my mama's family. For generations McQueen women have been baking pecan pie. Long before Paula Deen opened her restaurant or had even thought of baking her first pie."

His smile widened, but he made note of something she had revealed, perhaps without realizing it. Kelly had mentioned her mother's family and the name McQueen. A slip of the tongue, no doubt, but it sounded as if there wasn't a dad in her life.

No reason for him to mention her family, so he moved on to a safer subject. "Love the watercolors in your living room. I was on temporary duty to Fort Stewart a number of times and always headed to Savannah for shrimp and grits."

"No étouffée? You sound more like a Southern boy than a Cajun."

"Yeah, well, I've worked hard to get rid of my New Orleans roots."

She paused to stare at him, her brow raised. "Really?"

He cleared his throat and shrugged, realizing too late he had said more than he should have. "I said goodbye to the Big Easy when I was twelve and moved to the small town of DeRidder, Lousiana."

"Near Fort Polk?"

"That's right. Lots of good army folks lived in the area, so as I got older, going into the military seemed to be a good decision."

"And your accent?"

"My aunt was an English teacher. She went to school up north and was a stickler for proper pronunciation."

"So no *who dat* or *fais do-do* or *laissez les bon temps rouler?*"

"Ah, *ma chère.*" He laughed. "It don madda no more."

"Which is something my father used to say." Her smile vanished. "Actually anything that mattered to me never mattered to him."

So there was a dad. "Was he from New Orleans?"

"I'm afraid so." She turned back to the coffee, but he could see tension in the way she held her shoulders. Evidently, mention of Kelly's dad was something to be avoided.

"So what about you?" He threw out the question hoping to steer the conversation in a better direction. "Is Savannah home?"

"It was." She glanced around. "Now this place claims that distinction."

"Have you been back recently?"

The light in her eyes faded. "A couple weeks ago." She paused for a moment as the coffee dripped into the carafe. Once again, he had treaded into difficult waters.

She took a deep breath. "My mother passed away. I went home to bury her."

"Oh, Kelly, I'm sorry."

"She had been in the local nursing home for the last year, so it wasn't unexpected."

"Still, it's a terrible loss."

Kelly pulled two mugs from the cabinet. "I moved her here when her condition took a turn for the worse. She needed long-term care, and I wanted to be close so I could check on her often. The nursing home is just a short drive down the road."

"I remember passing it tonight. Magnolia Gardens?"

"That's right. Luckily a bed opened up just when mom needed one. At the time, I lived in the bachelor officer quarters on post. When this house went on the market, I decided to move."

"I'm sure your mother appreciated all you did for her."

Kelly's gaze was pensive. "I'm not sure. My mother…" She bit her lip and hesitated for a moment. "Mom wasn't one to show her appreciation, but being close to her made me feel useful. That at least I was doing something to care for her needs."

She placed a sugar bowl on the small table and pulled a pitcher of milk from the refrigerator, which she placed next to the sugar. "I admire Lola Taylor for taking care of her mother-in-law this past year while her husband was deployed."

Phil heard the regret in Kelly's voice. "You couldn't have cared for your mom without help. We both know being in the military is a 24/7 commitment."

"You're right, but it still bothers me."

"What about Savannah? Was there anyone else to help with her care? A sister or brother?"

"I'm an only child."

"And your dad?"

"He died when I was fifteen."

"Tough, huh?"

Turning back to the coffeepot, she failed to comment. Instead, she poured the fresh brew into the two mugs and handed one to him. "Milk or sugar?"

"Black's fine."

Retrieving a knife and serving spatula from the drawer, she placed the utensils on the table next to two plates. "How about some pie?"

"Nothing could stop me from saying yes."

She cut into the flaky crust and placed a large piece on a plate. The rich sugary interior spilled out like amber gold.

Phil's mouth watered. How long had it been since he'd last eaten? Too long.

"Kelly, I have to tell you, nothing has looked this good in a long time."

She laughed. The warm sound echoed in the kitchen and made Phil realize this woman standing before him wasn't the cold ice queen interested only on the next CID case. She baked, for goodness's sake.

He slipped his fork into the delectable richness and pulled a huge chunk into his open mouth. His eyes closed, and he sighed with contentment.

"Mmm, this is to die for." He licked his lips and opened his eyes in time to see Kelly staring at him.

"You're easy to satisfy, Captain." She grabbed the pot and refreshed his cup.

"And your coffee's strong, *ma chère,* the way I like it."

She stopped on her way back to the coffeemaker. "Seems a bit of the Cajun is still in your blood, Captain."

"I guess old habits die hard." He laughed, but when she didn't, he stuck another bite into his mouth and washed it down with the hot coffee. "I love this pie."

In all likelihood, Kelly McQueen didn't cotton—as they say in the South—to Cajuns. A fact he needed to remember.

"What time do you expect to get to the company tomorrow?" he asked, once again redirecting her attention to something other than his Louisiana roots.

"Early. I'd like to start talking to the men individually, which will take time. Then as soon as the autopsy is completed, Jamison is slated to pick up the spent round and transport it along with the rifles to our lab at Fort Gillam."

"I'll let the executive officer know. He'll ensure the weapons are signed over to either you or Jamison to maintain the chain of custody. He can also assign some men to help transport them."

"That won't be necessary. Jamison and a couple of the other CID guys plan to accompany the weapons to Gillam in a military vehicle."

Phil raised his brow but said nothing. He understood her desire to keep extra personnel from interfering in her investigation. If their jobs were reversed, Phil would be equally as cautious about outsiders muddying up the process.

"What about the kid you saw on the street?" he asked.

"If the local police can't find him, I'll call his stepmother and see if he's staying with her. Maybe she knows why he's back."

"Probably to see that girlfriend you mentioned."

"Maybe. Hopefully, Mrs. Foglio will know how I can contact the girl. I'll also want to find out who owns the land that butts up to the Taylor's place."

"Let me know if you uncover anything." He took a last bite of the pie and carried his plate and mug to the sink. After rinsing the dishes, he placed them in the dishwasher.

"Looks like your mother trained you well." Kelly smiled.

"My aunt," he reminded her.

"My mistake."

Now Kelly was the one who looked embarrassed.

"Aunt Eleanor was a God-fearing woman who ensured I always cleaned up after myself." Phil smiled at Kelly, hoping to reassure her before he glanced at his watch. "She also told me never to overstay my welcome. Thanks for the coffee and pie."

"Anytime."

"I also like peach cobbler and bread pudding."

"Why, Captain." Kelly exaggerated her drawl. "You really sound like a good ole Southern boy."

He grabbed his beret off the table and joined in her levity. "But, ma'am, Louisiana *is* the South."

"Why sure 'nuff it is, Jean Philippe."

Her use of his full name caught him off guard. His mother had called him Jean Philippe. The memory warmed him for an instant until the bitterness returned. How could he feel anything for a woman who cared more about her job than her young son?

Moving toward the living room, Phil stopped short when he heard the garage door close. He glanced back at Kelly. "Are you expecting someone?"

She shook her head, then opened the kitchen door and peered into the garage. Phil put his arm protectively on her shoulder and stepped around her. His gaze flicked over the interior of the car illuminated by the light from the automatic opener.

"Maybe someone else has the same code your system uses on their own remote," he suggested.

"Maybe. But I didn't hear a car drive by."

Nor had Phil. "I'll take a look around before I head back to Rickman."

"I hate to put you out."

"Not a problem." He made a wide sweep around the house and grounds, but saw nothing that seemed unusual. Kelly was standing on the step when he returned to the front of the house.

"Everything looks okay," he said to reassure her.

"Thanks for checking." She patted her right leg. "If it weren't for the swelling, I would have done it myself."

Kelly's house stood alone on a desolate stretch of road. Phil glanced once again at the dense wooded area to the side and rear of her property.

The Magnolia Gardens nursing home was only a couple hundred yards away to the south, but other than the long-term care facility, Kelly was pretty much on her own.

"Have you ever thought about getting a couple floodlights for the backyard? Dead bolts on your doors would help."

"Security hasn't been an issue, Phil." She tilted her head. "Besides, I'm a good shot."

He nodded. "Top marksman on post is what I heard."

"Top marksman in law enforcement. There are plenty of other good marksmen on post. I'm one of many."

"I doubt that. From what I heard, you're being a bit too modest."

"Humility has never been my strong suit." She smiled. "Now don't worry. I'll be fine."

He slapped his beret against his pants' leg. He knew it was time to get going, but he hated to leave her.

She turned to enter her house and then glanced over her shoulder. "See you in the morning, Phil."

He walked slowly back to his truck. Dawn would come soon enough. He needed sleep to clear his head and override his desire to camp out on her front step. For some reason, he had an overwhelming desire to stand guard throughout the night.

As he climbed into his truck, he glanced once again at the small brick ranch. A light went on in a window on the far side of the house. While he was wondering if she'd be okay, Kelly was, no doubt, thinking of anything except the army captain who had needed a cup of coffee and a piece of pie.

There wasn't room for their personal interests to get in the way of the job they needed to do. Kelly probably felt the same way he did, and for some reason, that bothered him.

FIVE

Kelly glanced out the window as Phil steered his pickup onto the main road and headed back to Freemont. As she watched, his taillights disappeared into the distance. A sense of isolation she had experienced following her mother's death returned to wrap around her shoulders. The house seemed too quiet and the night too dark.

While Phil had been in her kitchen, she hadn't felt that way. In fact, she'd enjoyed seeing him eat the pie chased with coffee, and she was thankful she had invited him inside.

He seemed like a nice guy, even if he was a Cajun at heart. Surely he wasn't shiftless and deceptive like her father had been. Still, she wouldn't allow herself to let down her guard.

She was tired tonight, which was probably the reason her emotions were so volatile. In the morning, she would see things in a different light.

Phil didn't want to think about Kelly or Lola Taylor and her mother-in-law. He wanted to crawl into bed and fall blissfully to sleep. Maybe it was because of Taylor's death or because he'd been in the field for so long, but today had sapped his energy.

He worked hard to ensure the company accomplished each

mission it was given. Today, the mission had failed with terrible consequences. The need to make things right was foremost on his mind. As soon as he grabbed some shut-eye, he had to find out what had gone wrong and fix it. But he couldn't fix the fact that Corporal Taylor had died.

Although Lola Taylor had practically escorted them to the door earlier, Phil knew she shouldn't be alone tonight. She had mentioned her mother-in-law. From what he'd seen of Mildred Taylor, she wouldn't offer the younger woman the support she needed.

A number of the company commanders felt their responsibility extended no further than the soldiers in their units. Phil believed his circle of concern extended to the families, as well. Tired though he was, he couldn't go back to post until he ensured Lola Taylor was able to cope with her grief and getting the support she needed.

Magnolia Gardens appeared on the left, a single-story brick building with various wings that trailed off from the central string of rooms. He pulled into the parking lot, drove by the front entrance and circled around, exiting back onto the two-lane road, but this time headed north.

He slowed down as he passed Kelly's place. The lights were still on inside, but the surrounding yard sat cloaked in darkness.

She really was isolated and far from any neighbors. A couple of floodlights might help to deter anyone from approaching the lone dwelling in the middle of the night.

As competent as Kelly seemed, and while she was convinced she could take care of herself, a few precautions would make Phil feel a lot better about her safety.

He glanced at the odometer, mentally making note of the mileage, and increased his speed as he rounded the curve and lost sight of her property. He covered the five additional

miles to the farmhouse in good time without seeing another
car on the road, once again confirming Kelly's isolation.

In the distance, he noticed the Taylor mailbox and drive.
The lights in the house were still on, and a pickup truck—a
dually extended cab—sat parked next to the house. At this
distance, he couldn't make out the make or model, but as he
neared, light from the porch spilled over the enclosed truck
bed, which was light-colored, either white or beige. A reflective sticker was visible on the right rear bumper. A circle of
some sort, not unlike the unit crest decal Phil had on the back
of his own truck.

Maybe one of the wives in the unit was comforting Mrs.
Taylor. Relieved to know she wasn't alone, Phil turned
around at the next widening of the road. He wouldn't disturb Mrs. Taylor and the Good Samaritan who had come to
offer support.

At least he could now return to post and get some sleep
knowing Lola Taylor was in good hands. But as he drove by
Kelly McQueen's house, he realized he couldn't feel as confident about the CID agent.

He'd talk to her again tomorrow about installing bolts
on her doors and floodlights to illuminate the backyard.
He would also talk to her about her own safety, although
he didn't know if she would take his advice. She seemed
confident in her ability, and rightfully so. Kelly was a competent CID agent who seemed to tackle her job with determination.

She was totally focused on the investigation, which was
as it should be. Phil, on the other hand, had a problem. Sepa-
rating the CID agent McQueen from the pretty blonde who
made him go into protective mode when she was near was a
problem he needed to correct.

There was no reason he should think of Kelly McQueen

as anything except a competent special agent, yet her blond hair and big blue eyes kept getting in the way.

Kelly opened the dishwasher and placed her own mug and dirty plate in the rack, next to where Phil had placed his. Nice guy to think of loading the dishwasher with his dirty dishes. He'd mentioned an aunt, but not a mother.

She had always thought of him as growing up in a privileged home, especially when she would see him at the club. Invariably, he was surrounded by women who had money and status stamped on their designer clothes. When she was a girl, her mother used to talk about the folks who lived in the beautiful old homes in the historic district.

"Can't you just imagine what it would be like living in those fine homes, Kelly Ann?" she'd say as they walked along the sidewalk. "Honey, those folks don't know trouble. Everything comes easy to them that have money." She would then mention her own family coming from a long line of prestigious Southerners who had somehow lost their wealth but not their lineage.

When Kelly was hungry and left alone because her mom worked two jobs to put food on the table, she could have cared less about the prestigious line into which she had been born. She was more concerned about how her mother would pay the electric bill and whether the canned goods in the cupboard could be stretched until the next paycheck.

Maybe Phil's life had had a few rough spots, as well. The military was a good equalizer. No matter where a person came from or what their situation had been, once they swore an oath of allegiance to the United States and put on the uniform, what they had been or where they had come from no longer mattered.

Except Phil was a sweet-talking Cajun, which remained a

problem. Luckily, their relationship was totally professional. Once the investigation was over, their paths would part.

Leaving the kitchen, Kelly heard a vehicle drive by on the road. Pulling back the drapes ever so slightly, she glanced at the taillights heading back to town. The pickup truck looked familiar. So did the reflective unit crest on the rear of the cab. Phil?

Had he doubled back to the farmhouse? And if so, why?

As she crawled into bed later that night, Kelly couldn't stop wondering what he had been doing. Just as her body relaxed and she drifted to sleep, the rumble of her garage door startled her awake. Reaching for her gun with one hand, she pulled back the covers with the other and stepped onto the carpet, every muscle on alert.

Easing back the bedroom curtain, she stared into the darkness outside. Her gaze took in the driveway and the two-lane road void of taillights or headlights or anything that indicated a passing vehicle.

Weapon in hand, she left her bedroom and slowly made her way along the hall. Pausing at the entrance to the living room, Kelly scanned the room. The drapes were still drawn and the furnishings as she had left them. The tiny light inside the curio cabinet in the corner illuminated her mother's teacup collection. The cups and saucers were intricately hand painted and trimmed with Florentine gold. Although Kelly doubted they would be worth much monetarily, they were priceless to her.

Moving slowly into the dining area and then the kitchen beyond, she continued to listen for the sound of an intruder. Instead she heard the hum of the refrigerator and the movement of water as the ice maker filled.

The garage door had never malfunctioned since it had been installed eight months ago. Now in one night, the door had unexpectedly activated twice.

Pretty common to find duplicate systems programmed to work on the same frequency, which could cause a problem if another person clicked their remote as they drove by her house. Although that seemed unlikely. Still, it was an explanation, and the best one she could come up with at the moment.

Squaring her shoulders, she reached for the kitchen door and eased it open. The overhead light bathed the garage in light.

Glancing quickly around, she let out the breath she had been holding. Nothing was waiting on the other side of the door except cold air and her car. Still gripping her weapon, Kelly stepped into the open garage and glanced out at the front yard.

Wind blew through the tall pines and sturdy hardwood trees. The eerie sound and the chilly night air sent a shiver down her spine. Shrugging off her concern, she turned to go back inside and pushed the button to lower the garage door.

As it started to engage, her gaze swept the interior of her Corolla. Something caught her eye. Kelly leaned down to take a closer look.

A length of thick hemp was wrapped around her steering wheel. One end of the rope had been cut in two. The opposite end was tied in the noose—the same noose that had wrapped around her ankle earlier tonight.

The hair on her neck rose in protest as the garage door slammed shut behind her. She jumped at the sound. Her left hand flew to her heart, which pounded hard against her chest.

Had Kyle Foglio followed her home and placed the rope in her car? Or was someone else trying to scare her?

SIX

The next morning, Kelly entered post through the main gate well before dawn and passed Phil's headquarters on her way to the live-fire training range. One lone streetlight illuminated the small parking area near the bleachers where she left her car.

The temperature had dropped in the night, and she pulled her blue windbreaker closed to keep the cold at bay. A layer of frost crusted the ground and crunched underfoot as she walked across the barren terrain.

She should have brought gloves. Her hands felt stiff from the cold, and she rubbed them together, hoping to increase circulation.

Approaching the crime scene, she envisioned how the platoon had spread out in formation as they advanced toward the rise. Cresting the hill, she spied a wooden target in the distance. The so-called objective had been cut out of plywood to symbolize an enemy armored personnel carrier.

She neared the target and examined the rounds that had found their mark. Before she turned to retrace her steps, the sound of footfalls signaled she wasn't alone.

Her neck tingled a warning. Common knowledge the guilty often returned to the scene of the crime.

Kelly reached for her gun. Stiff though they were, her fingers wrapped around the cold steel handle as she turned to face the approaching visitor.

A form in the darkness drew closer.

Kelly aimed her gun. "Disturb my crime scene and I'll haul you into the stockade faster than you can say *Uncle Sam.*"

The figure stopped dead in his tracks as the first rays of light broke over the horizon.

"Do you always pull your weapon on unsuspecting soldiers?"

Kelly let out the breath she had been holding. "Only when they sneak up on me in the dark. What are you doing here, Phil?"

"Trying to find you. I saw you drive by the company and attempted to flag you down. Evidently, you didn't see me waving my arms."

"Flag me down? For what reason?"

"To tell you I'd made a pot of coffee and stopped at the bakery on post for doughnuts. I thought you might be hungry."

"You followed me all the way out here just to tell me the coffee's on?"

He nodded. "My Aunt Eleanor always said a man needed to start the day with his belly full."

Kelly let out a frustrated breath and shook her head. "Well, in case you haven't noticed, I'm a woman, and my belly does not need to be perpetually full."

She holstered her weapon. "But coffee sounds good, and I doubt I'll find anything in the dark that I didn't see yesterday. The temperature must be hovering around the freezing mark."

"Twenty-nine degrees a couple of hours ago when I came to work."

"Didn't you leave my house a couple hours ago?"

"Six hours to be exact. Long enough to catch a few winks of shut-eye and then shower and change uniforms. I don't know how the CID handles short nights, but I'm good to go."

"And I will be after coffee. But first, I need to know what you did last night after you left my place."

"You must have seen me pass your house." He stamped the ground with his feet. "I was concerned about Mrs. Taylor being alone and drove back to the farmhouse. I'm not sure if I planned to knock on her door or just salve my conscience that she was okay."

He shrugged. "Turns out a beige pickup truck was parked outside. A decal that looked like our unit crest was on the back bumper, so I'm pretty sure one of the wives must have visited her."

"That's good. I was worried about her, too."

Phil pointed to where Kelly had parked her car. "We might be more comfortable discussing everything at my company headquarters."

"I'll follow you."

Together they hustled to their vehicles and met up back at the company. Phil motioned her into his office. Although not large, the room was big enough for a good-size desk and two comfortable chairs. Kelly settled into one of the chairs while Phil headed for the small table in the corner that held the coffeepot. The rich aroma of the fresh brew filled the room.

"Cream or sugar?"

"A little of each, thanks."

Phil fixed a cup and took it to Kelly before he opened a box of doughnuts on his desk and offered them to her, along with a paper plate and napkin.

"I'm impressed. You think of everything. Must be Aunt Eleanor's influence." She placed two doughnuts on her plate and took a bite of one before she noticed powdered sugar had fallen onto her lap. Brushing it off, she smiled. "I seem to be making a mess."

Despite her tough-as-nails CID facade, when the special agent let her guard down, she had a charming demeanor he found enticing.

"I told my executive officer to gather the men together so you and I can talk to each soldier individually, after we visit Lola Taylor."

"That works for me."

"I knew you would want to review the live-fire operations order from yesterday's exercise." Phil handed her a file from a folder on his desk. "My platoon leaders and the battalion staff have reviewed the op order. No one sees anything that could have led to the training accident."

"So you're convinced it was an accident?"

"Yes, but I'm counting on you to determine the how and why."

She nodded. "Hopefully, I'll have that information by the end of the investigation."

When she finished the doughnuts, she wiped the napkin over her mouth. "I called the local authorities on my way to post and talked to an officer named Tim Simpson. He hasn't been in town long and wasn't sure who owned the land adjacent to the Taylor property, but he said he'd make some inquiries."

"Excellent."

"He did mention a campsite located about half a mile from the main road. An old geezer used to hole up out there in a broken-down trailer."

"Have they seen him recently?"

"The neighbor to the south heard a volley of shots a couple months back and notified the police. When they arrived at the campsite, the trailer was deserted. As far as they know, the old guy has never returned."

"Did they suspect foul play?"

"No one issued a missing-persons report."

"Might behoove us to take a drive out there and see what we can find."

Kelly nodded. "Then afterward we can talk to the two Mrs. Taylors."

A knock sounded on the door, and Chaplain Sanchez peered inside. "You mentioned coffee and doughnuts?"

"Come in, Chaplain." Phil filled a foam cup and pointed out the cardboard container of creamer and the sugar packets. "I'll let you doctor it up to your own taste. Help yourself to the doughnuts."

"Appreciate it, Phil."

"How are the men this morning?" Kelly asked as the chaplain fixed his coffee and gobbled down a doughnut.

Phil settled into the chair behind his desk. "It's a tough call. Sleep helped, but their morale's at rock bottom."

"I talked to Stanley." The chaplain took a sip of his coffee. "From the way he looked, he must have been awake all night. I prayed with him and that seemed to help. On my way out of the barracks, I ran into Sergeant Gates."

"He's Stanley's squad leader," Phil informed Kelly.

"Gates called him impetuous," the chaplain shared.

Phil reached for a doughnut. "Actually, he's a good kid, but he sometimes acts before he thinks. Of course, I could say the same thing about a number of the soldiers in the company."

The chaplain nodded. "Probably so. At least Stanley knows the Lord. That goes a long way."

"Any idea of the value of the Taylor land?" Kelly asked.

"From the number of new home sites going in around the area, land values have to be going up." Phil scooted back in his chair. "The army's slated to send more troops to Rickman next year, and more housing will be needed to accommodate the growing number of military families in the area."

The chaplain reached for a second doughnut. "What are you getting at, Kelly?"

"Lola said her husband was an only child, so the farmhouse and surrounding land would have gone to Corporal Taylor upon his mother's death. Now the property will go to his widow."

Phil wrinkled his brow. "You mean when Mildred passes on?"

"Exactly." Kelly nodded. "We need to keep our eyes open."

Phil shook his head. "But that has nothing to do with Corporal Taylor's death, Kelly."

"How do you know that? I want to learn more about Corporal Taylor. His mother. His father. Anything could have bearing on the investigation."

Phil frowned. "His dad died a few years ago."

"Actually, Kelly's got a point." The chaplain took a final swig of his coffee. "It's a known fact that fathers play an important role in their children's lives. Studies have even shown that a person's relationship with the Lord is based on how his or her father viewed God."

"But we're not focusing on Taylor's religious beliefs, Chaplain."

"No, but that paternal influence has to play into other areas of a person's life, as well. The virtues they espouse, their own feelings of self-worth, their work ethic and determination to provide for their families are all impacted by how they view their father."

Phil pursed his lips. He couldn't read Kelly's expression. Yesterday, he had gotten the impression her relationship with her dad had been less than ideal.

"What about a mother's influence?" Kelly asked.

"In most cases, the mother remains with the children, even in a divorce situation, so she continues to be a steadying influence in her children's lives."

Phil bristled. "Sounds as if we're we discussing sociology issues instead of the Taylor family." He glanced at his watch and then eyed Kelly. "How 'bout an early-morning drive? We can check out the deserted trailer and then stop by the farmhouse."

"You bet." She rose and placed her mug near the coffeepot.

He noticed her limp. "What about the leg?"

"A bit swollen, but it'll get better with time."

"Sick call runs until 0900 hours. We could postpone the trip until you see the doc."

"I'm okay, Phil."

He turned to the chaplain. "Care to join us?"

"Thanks, but no. I'll hang around the company in case anyone else needs to talk." His cell rang. Pulling the phone from his pocket, he flipped it open and raised it to his ear.

"This is Chaplain Sanchez." He nodded, listening to the caller. "Tell him I'll be there in five minutes."

The chaplain closed his phone. "Lieutenant Colonel Knowlton wants to see me."

A warning flag went off in Phil's mind. "About the investigation?"

"I'm not sure. He knows I've been talking to the men and probably wants my impression on how they're doing."

The muscle in Phil's neck twitched. "Which I could have discussed with him, as well."

"No reason to be on the defensive, Phil. He's looking for answers, that's all." The chaplain patted Phil's shoulder. "The Lord provides. Put your trust in Him. He'll take care of you and the men."

"Your confidence in the Divine is a little late in coming, Chaplain. If the Lord had been on my side, Corporal Taylor would still be alive."

"Unfortunately, we don't know the reason why bad things happen, but scripture assures us that all things work for good. Hold on to that promise." Sanchez threw the empty cup into the trash can. "Thanks for the coffee."

Once he had left, Phil grabbed his beret and motioned Kelly toward the door. "Did you buy into what the chaplain said?"

"The part about fathers and their children, or his suggestion that you turn to the Lord?"

"Both."

"I put my trust in my weapon and my own ability."

"What about your father?"

"He wasn't in my life long enough to have any influence on me."

Phil couldn't say the same. Everything he'd done since he was twelve had been to prove he was a better man than his father had been. At this moment, he wondered if what he had believed for the past seventeen years had been a lie.

SEVEN

"Law enforcement. CID from Fort Rickman."

Kelly knocked on the door of the deserted trailer, her right hand on her weapon. A side window had been patched with plywood and duct tape. One of the tires was flat.

She hesitated for a moment and then reached for the handle and inched the door open.

"Careful," Phil cautioned.

Her gaze flicked right and then left to ensure no one was inside before she climbed the steps. The interior was small and smelled musty.

Glancing at the trash can, she noticed a fast-food wrapper and a portion of a hamburger bun. "Looks like someone's been here recently."

Phil stood beside her, taking up much of the confined area. The hair on her neck tingled with his nearness, and she took a step back to put space between them.

The washroom door stood closed. Kelly pulled her gun and eased it open. A shirt hung on a hook on the back of the door. Using the tip of her weapon, she laid the shirt on a nearby counter. The front was torn and spattered with blood.

"The kid from last night?" Phil asked.

"Looks like it. He must be staying here. What made those cuts in the fabric?"

Phil shook his head. "I don't have a clue, but whoever attacked the kid kept jabbing at him."

"Let's take a look around." Once outside, Kelly pointed to a path that cut into the woods. "It has to go someplace, right?"

With long strides, Phil moved ahead of her, and she struggled to catch up. His gaze scanned the landscape like a good officer scouting out the terrain. She should be doing the same, but her eyes kept returning to his long legs and the strength of his muscular arms. She couldn't help but remember the sense of security she'd felt in his embrace last night.

Her world had turned upside down, and evidently, her judgment had, as well. Phil Thibodeaux was the least likely man to show up on her radar. If she were looking for Mr. Right, which she wasn't, he wouldn't be a Cajun.

Phil stopped and turned, evidently realizing she was having difficulty keeping up with him. His face broke into an apologetic grin. "I forgot about your leg."

Sunlight danced across his ruddy cheeks and his lips opened ever so slightly as he stared down at her. She noted the flecks of gold in his twinkling eyes.

"Look, I'm okay. Besides, you taped it last night and the bandage is still in place."

She noted the combat infantry badge on his chest and the Ranger tab on his shoulder. Both put him above and beyond in regards to combat readiness and the ability to handle any emergency. Even a twisted ankle.

"Somehow I don't believe you." His gaze penetrated hers with an intensity that left her light-headed.

She averted her eyes and glanced at where the path disappeared into the woods. "Could you slow down once we get to the wooded area?"

He smiled, revealing the dimples, which sent another wave

of instability rumbling through her body. So much for being in control.

"Ladies first." He gestured her forward. "You set the pace and I'll follow."

Knowing Phil was behind her made her stomach flutter whenever she thought of those dimples and the glint of warmth from his eyes. Luckily, the brush was dense, which forced her to focus on the path that eventually led to a smaller clearing.

A sense of déjà vu swept over Kelly as she stared at the thick trunk of the sturdy oak where she had hung last night. She turned to glance at Phil. "I wasn't far from the trailer."

He stepped forward and swept away the fallen leaves at the base of the tree with his boot.

"Looking for the rope?" She pulled a plastic evidence bag containing the cut edge of the thick hemp from her coat pocket. "I found this in my car when my garage door opened in the middle of the night."

"Did you call the police?"

"I am law enforcement, Phil."

"The local cops needed to know what happened, Kelly. I can't believe you didn't call them."

"It was late. They would have taken a statement and looked around. I didn't want them traipsing around my property."

He stepped closer and stared down at her. "You're too isolated in that house, Kelly. Have you thought about moving back to the bachelor officer's quarters on post? Or you could get a room at the Post Lodge for a few days until this all blows over."

"Kyle Foglio doesn't frighten me." She pointed to her holster. "Plus, I've got a gun."

"What's his story, Kelly?"

"He was a troubled kid. Then his dad went to jail. His

mother has other interests than parenting, and his relationship with his stepmom isn't the best. She had enough on her plate when her husband went to jail. Things might be different now, but I bet Kyle isn't willing to step back into that environment."

"So he's striking out at you instead?"

"I'm the first one who hauled him in for questioning a couple of years ago when he came to live with his dad. He got into trouble and didn't stay long on post."

"Because of your intervention?"

"Because of the pressure put to bear on his father by the commanding general."

"The big guns came out. You did that?"

"No, but Kyle might think I'm the reason. Nate Patterson was the lead investigator on his father's case. I was in Savannah at the time caring for my mother, who was in the hospital."

"Before you brought her back to the nursing home in Freemont?"

"That's right. In the kid's opinion, I'm probably the one who gave him the most grief."

"So he comes after you?" Phil glanced around the clearing. "Is it a coincidence that he ends up hiding out on property next to the Taylors' farmhouse?"

A cold wind broke through the clearing and sent a chill down Kelly's spine. "I learned early on that there are no coincidences when you're dealing with a crime."

They hiked back to his pickup, and Phil helped Kelly into the passenger seat, knowing full well she was in pain. "You need to have someone look at that injury. An X-ray would be a good idea, as well."

"Sounds like you're hoping to get rid of me and have a new special agent assigned to your case." She laughed as he slid behind the wheel and started the engine. The light, female sound made his lips curl into a smile and the tension in his shoulders ease a bit.

He was suddenly enjoying himself. "Don't you think I like driving all over the outlying area of Freemont with a pretty blonde at my side? Most people say I'm wound too tight. They'll get a different impression of me when they see me taking time off from the job to be with you."

"Wound too tight? I've heard you're a ladies' man who enjoys tall and lanky women who are low on intellect and high on beauty."

"Now that's a sexist comment if I ever heard one."

She huffed playfully. "Sexist?"

"Do you always believe everything you hear?"

"Didn't you have an attractive date for the military ball a couple months ago?"

"Aha! You were watching me." His eyes twinkled as he glanced at her.

"I was not." Her cheeks warmed as she tried to backtrack, which made him want to laugh even more loudly. The cute CID agent was actually squirming in her seat.

Kelly wrapped her arms over her chest and raised her chin with determination. "As I recall, you were two tables over from me. Most of the guys at my table couldn't keep their eyes off your date."

"Funny." Phil pulled his gaze back to the road. "I thought they were drooling over you."

Kelly sat up straighter. "You have no idea what you're talking about, Captain."

He stole a glance at her profile and noticed the red streak of embarrassment that rose from her neck. Seems Ms. Put Together CID Agent had trouble with her own self-image.

Some of her false bravado must be just that.

If truth be told, he enjoyed working with Kelly. She was

smart and savvy and determined. All qualities he admired. Plus, she made him laugh.

He thought of the young punk who was undoubtedly causing her problems. Suddenly another feeling settled over him—a chilling realization that Kelly might be in danger.

He glanced at her once again as she looked out the window. He'd do everything he could to keep her safe.

EIGHT

"I'd like to talk to your mother-in-law." Kelly and Phil stood on Lola Taylor's front porch. The widow had opened her door a few inches and seemed hesitant to let them in.

Lola's eyes were clear, and her face didn't have the lines of fatigue Kelly had expected to see. From all indications, she seemed to have had a decent night's sleep and was facing this particular Wednesday with a good outlook. Yet appearances could be deceiving. Kelly knew that for sure.

Most people thought she was put-together and hard-core. If they realized some of her own internal struggle, they might think otherwise. Her father's caustic words of disapproval often circled in her head. He had been so careful to never utter them when her mother was around. Not that it would have mattered. Her mom looked through the eyes of love that were clouded by what she wanted to see instead of the reality of what really was.

"Your survival assistance officer should be contacting you soon to set up an appointment." Phil peered around Kelly. "In the meantime, I wanted to check your husband's insurance paperwork before the request for payment is submitted."

"There won't be a problem with the policy, will there?" Lola asked.

"No, ma'am. But I would like to talk to you about what still needs to be done."

The widow finally seemed convinced that inviting the company commander and CID agent into her home would work to her advantage. Lola opened the door and let them in. Kelly smelled eggs and bacon and wondered if the widow had made breakfast for her mother-in-law.

"While you and the captain talk, I'll visit with Mildred," Kelly said as Lola closed the door behind them.

"She's sleeping." The widow's tone was firm.

"Perhaps I could just sit with her."

"I really don't think that's necessary."

Kelly reached for Lola's hand and offered a compassionate smile. "My own mother died just a couple weeks ago, Mrs. Taylor. I promise I won't disturb Mildred, but I would like to see her again."

"I'm sorry about your loss, Agent McQueen. You must understand how I feel."

"I won't do anything to upset Mildred. I promise."

Before Lola could reply, a faint cry came from the rear of the house. "Sounds like she's awake."

The widow shrugged. "She probably heard the knock at the door. I'll check on her."

"Please," Kelly insisted. "I just want to say hello."

Lola bristled and pulled her hand back. Then she relaxed a bit. "I haven't told her about Rick."

"I won't mention his death."

Kelly followed Lola along the hallway to the small bedroom at the rear of the house. The blinds were drawn, and the room seemed stuffy.

Mildred's face cracked into a crooked smile when she saw Kelly. Her eyes, which had seemed clear last night, now appeared rheumy and clouded.

"Mother Taylor, I have breakfast warming in the kitchen

when you feel up to eating." Lola fluffed her pillow. "She's having a bad morning, as you can see. Some days are better than others. Recently, she's taken a turn for the worse. The doctor says her condition is deteriorating."

"Is her doctor in Freemont?"

"Actually, there's a geriatric clinic that handles cases like hers. It's in a nearby town."

"Garfield?" Kelly offered the name of the clinic she had used for her own mother. Lola shook her head but failed to offer more information as Mildred closed her eyes and slipped back to sleep.

Kelly pulled a chair closer to the bed. "Why don't you talk to Captain Thibodeaux, and I'll sit with your mother-in-law."

Lola's brow furrowed, but finally the widow shrugged. "Call me if she wakes. She needs to eat."

"Of course."

Lola returned to the living room where Kelly could hear her talking with Phil. She picked up a bottle of pills off the nightstand that held sleeping tablets. Another contained ibuprofen.

Kelly pulled open the small drawer on the bedside table and found an empty bottle crammed all the way in the back, the pharmacy label was made out to Mildred Taylor. Thirty caplets of oxycodone.

The high-strength pain medication had been prescribed by Dr. Addison Kutter and filled at the Kutter Geriatric Clinic Pharmacy, although the label failed to provide an address or phone number for the facility. The date confirmed the prescription had been filled less than a week ago, but the bottle was empty.

Kelly scooted closer to the old woman and looked down at her face. The lines of concern that furrowed her brow when she was awake had relaxed, and Mrs. Taylor seemed at peace.

"What's going on, Mildred?" Kelly whispered.

A doctor had prescribed oxycodone for pain, yet when Mildred had seemed distraught, Lola had given her mother-in-law an over-the-counter sleeping medication.

"I know you haven't had time to decide on funeral arrangements," Phil said to Lola as Kelly returned to the living room. "The wives in the company would like to host a lunch following the service. They'd also like to provide meals for you and your mother-in-law."

Lola glanced nervously from Phil to Kelly. "How very thoughtful, but since there's just the two of us, cooking isn't a problem. Plus, my mother-in-law has problems maintaining her sugar levels and requires a special diet."

Kelly stepped closer. "And her other condition?"

Lola rose from the couch in an obvious attempt to signal the visit was over. "Mildred suffers from osteoarthritis complicated with dementia, which you would no doubt realize if you spoke with her. She sometimes becomes delusional and suffers from bouts of paranoia that can go along with the dementia." Lola turned cold eyes on Kelly. "I'm sure you've heard of Sundowners syndrome."

Kelly nodded. "Where mental awareness and memory regress around the time the sun goes down each day."

"That's right." Mrs. Taylor stepped closer to Kelly.

"But you said she's better in the morning, which is why Captain Thibodeaux and I stopped by now. We wanted to ask her about the property to the south of her farm. Do you know who owns the land? Or do you have any idea who would have set traps on the property?"

"Hunters perhaps?" Lola shrugged and held up her hands. "I never heard Mildred discuss any neighbors."

"Did your husband mention anyone who seemed a bit strange?"

"Rick and I moved here only shortly before he deployed.

We were still honeymooners, Agent McQueen, when he left for Afghanistan. We weren't talking about who lived where."

"Of course. Again, please accept my heartfelt sympathy."

Phil walked to where Kelly stood, and the two of them followed Lola to the door.

"I was stationed at Fort Knox early in my career." Kelly smiled warmly. "Were you from the area? Radcliff or Elizabethtown perhaps?"

"My home was in Vine Grove."

"Nice town," Kelly said before Phil shook Lola's hand.

"Will you have relatives coming for the funeral, Mrs. Taylor?" he asked.

"I'm not sure at this point."

"The company would like to help with transportation to and from the airport and with lodging reservations. As I mentioned earlier, the survival assistance officer will contact you later today."

"He'll call first?"

"Of course."

Kelly didn't say anything until she and Phil were both in the pickup. "Did anything hit you the wrong way?"

He glanced at her, their eyes locking. "She seems pretty much in control at this point. I would expect more signs of grief, but everyone faces the death of a loved one in a different way."

She nodded. "You're right."

"Okay, I'm waiting. I know there's a but."

"But—" Kelly shrugged "—Lola doesn't like people stopping by unannounced for one thing. She had a prescription for an addictive pain medication for her mother-in-law filled less than a week ago, yet the bottle is already empty."

"Maybe she uses dispensing containers that hold a week or two worth of pills in individual compartments. When my aunt got older, she used them to ensure she took the right pills on the right days."

Kelly sighed. "Maybe. I'm probably putting too much emphasis on her hesitancy to let me see Mildred."

"She reminds you of your mom, doesn't she?"

"Not in looks, but my mother was equally frail and debilitated before her death. The staff at the nursing home were wonderful, yet I still regret not being able to care for her in my home."

"Your work. How could you have held down a job and ensured your mother was all right? I doubt she could have stayed alone."

Kelly shook her head. "No, of course, not. Still…"

She glanced out the window as Phil turned the truck around. Something in the backyard caught her eye.

Kelly nudged Phil and pointed to four wire cages stacked next to a pile of cut firewood. "Are those chickens?"

Phil narrowed his gaze. "They look like roosters." He braked to a stop. "Let's check it out."

Nearing the pile of firewood, Kelly bent down and looked in the cages. "They're roosters, but their combs and wattles have been removed."

Phil nodded. "The birds have been dubbed. Their back spurs have been removed, as well. My guess, they've been raised as gamecocks."

"For fighting."

"Looks like it to me. Cockfighting was a problem in Louisiana—at least it was when I was a teen. My aunt was a forgiving woman, but there were a few people in town who were known to have been involved in cockfighting. Aunt Eleanor refused to speak to them even in church." He smiled at the memory. "She said there wasn't any good that could come from watching God's creatures fight to the death. Wasn't sport for sure and nothing to bet on. Not that she was a betting woman. Now, of course, cockfighting is illegal in Louisiana and most other states, as well."

The back door opened and Lola stepped onto the small cement step. "Is there a problem?"

Kelly and Phil both turned. "Not at all," Kelly said. "We were just admiring your roosters."

"They're not against the law."

Strange that she would instantly be on the defensive. But Lola was right. Having gamecocks was legal. However, betting on them or holding cockfights was not.

"Besides," the widow continued. "They belong to a neighbor. I'm keeping them until he comes back to town."

"A neighbor?" Kelly tilted her head. "But I thought you didn't know anyone around here."

"This gentleman lives outside of town to the east of Freemont. He should come to get his birds tonight."

"Interesting." Kelly turned and limped back to the pickup with Phil following close behind. Mrs. Taylor watched as they climbed into the truck and drove down the drive.

"She seemed concerned about us snooping around." Kelly glanced back and could see Lola still staring after them. "I wonder what she's trying to hide."

NINE

Phil's stomach growled. He looked up from the paperwork on his desk and glanced out the window. In the distance, the sky was darkening. Turning to face the clock on the wall, he was surprised to see it was already after 6:00 p.m. He and Kelly had grabbed a sandwich before noon, and both of them had been on the run ever since. No wonder his stomach was reminding him it was time for chow.

First Platoon's weapons had been signed over to Jamison Steele and had arrived at the CID ballistics lab at Fort Gillam, in the metro Atlanta area. Kelly had spent most of the afternoon interviewing the men one-on-one, until she had been called back to CID headquarters for a meeting, which should have been over by now.

Phil picked up the phone on his desk and called the CID office. "Is Kelly around?" he asked when Jamison answered.

"She left earlier for the pistol range. She wanted to get in some target practice before she headed home. A garage repairman was stopping by her house at the end of his workday to change her automatic opener. You heard about the problem she's been having?"

"I have to tell you, Jamison, it has me worried. Anyone entering that property unbidden in the middle of the night spells trouble."

"I agree. She's all alone on the edge of town, which has me worried, too."

"I'll drive out there and ensure the guy she hired is doing a good job. Do you know if she has plans for dinner?"

Jamison chuckled. "Is this a working dinner?"

"You bet. What else would it be?"

"Well…" The CID agent hesitated. "Kelly's a good-looking woman, and last I heard, you're a single guy."

"We're in the middle of an investigation."

"But that doesn't change the facts."

"I'm talking about a carry-out pizza, Jamison. Let's not make more out of this dinner than it warrants."

"I hear you. Enjoy yourself."

Phil couldn't help smiling. He liked Jamison, but the CID agent had put one and one together and gotten something very opposite of the real reason for Phil checking up on Kelly. Besides, they had more to discuss about the investigation, so, as Jamison had indicated, tonight would be a business meeting of sorts.

Which is what Phil kept telling himself as he picked up a large pizza, headed north along the Freemont Road and turned into Kelly's drive.

She must have heard him, because the garage door opened when he braked to a stop. Kelly came out from around her parked car. When she saw Phil, her face dropped. Suddenly he wasn't sure the pizza dinner was such a good idea.

"Hey." He climbed from the truck, then reached back inside for the pizza. "I brought dinner."

Her frown instantly turned upward. Evidently the saying about the best way to a guy's heart was through his stomach applied to women, as well. Not that Phil was interested, but he liked her smile.

She glanced at her watch. "I thought you were the garage

repairman. He said he'd be here at five o'clock. I called his shop about an hour ago, but the call went to voice mail."

"Maybe he got tied up on another job."

"You're probably right." Kelly led Phil through the garage and into the kitchen, where the smell of a scented candle and the sound of soft jazz eased the tension that had built up over the long day. If he ate slowly, maybe he could stay awhile and enjoy the ambiance of her home and her company.

She opened the pizza box on the counter and licked her lips. "How did you know I was starving? And pepperoni is my favorite."

He shrugged, totally pleased with himself. At least he'd done something right today.

Kelly pulled two colas from the fridge, and they sat at her kitchen table and chatted about nothing that had any bearing on the case, as if both of them wanted to distance themselves from the investigation.

He could get used to being with Kelly. The conversation flowed and they laughed, deep belly laughs that were therapeutic and refreshing. The fatigue that had weighed him down earlier disappeared, and instead he felt energized.

Kelly pulled out the last of the pecan pie and cut Phil a large slice, which he ate with relish. After helping her clear the table, he stuck the plates and glasses in the dishwasher. While she wiped off the table, he leaned against the counter.

"If anything good is to come from this investigation, Kelly, it's that I was able to finally meet you."

She dried her hands on a dish towel before glancing up at him. "You could have introduced yourself earlier, although people magnets, like you seem to be, never lack for friends."

Feeling put in his place, Phil raised his brow. "And now that you know me, what's your opinion?"

She leaned closer and wiped a crumb from the pie off his

upper lip. "Now I think you're a guy with a big heart who tries to live life by the book, but..."

"But what?" He pulled away from the counter, which placed him mere inches from her sweet mouth that suddenly wasn't smiling.

Instead, the expression on her face was full of anticipation, which probably matched the way his eyes were taking her in. The lift of her expressive brow, the glimmer of expectation that flickered in her eyes, the smoothness of her cheeks—now flushed and warm and almost iridescent—drew him closer.

Her hair, like strands of silk, cascaded over her shoulders. He ran his hand along a wayward strand before tucking it behind her ear. His fingers touched the flesh of her neck and sent pinpricks of electricity radiating up his arm.

Somewhere deep inside a voice warned of getting too close, but he wasn't listening as he focused on her lips and lowered his own to meet hers.

Before they made contact, the garage door activated.

Kelly turned to listen, her eyes wide, her body on alert. "Did you hear a car?"

He shook his head, his focus on the back door that led from the kitchen. "We didn't close the garage when we came inside. I'll go out the front and circle around."

She grabbed her weapon off the sideboard and headed for the kitchen door that led into the garage. Phil passed through the living area and inched the front door open. The porch light was off, and his eyes adjusted quickly to the surrounding darkness.

The yard was still, the road deserted.

He rounded the house to ensure no one was hovering in the rear. His eyes flicked over the wooded area. Floodlights were a priority. Kelly needed a lit backyard.

Expecting to see her at any moment, he circled the far side

of the house and rounded the corner to the garage. A warning went off in his head. Where was she?

At that moment, the automatic opener clicked into operation, and the garage door slowly rolled open.

The light from the overhead fixture spilled onto the driveway. Kelly stood just inside the garage on the cement slab. Her face was pulled tight, and her eyes were raised as she aimed her gun at the rafters.

Phil followed her gaze. His gut clenched and his spine tingled a warning. A dead possum hung from a noose above her car.

Kelly had forgotten to close her garage door when she and Phil had gone inside. Her mistake, a mistake that had given the perpetrator an opportunity to strike again.

This time his warning was even more unsettling.

"Kelly?" She turned as Phil stepped closer.

"I checked the rear of the house but didn't see anyone hanging around."

"How does he get in and out without me hearing?"

"The garage was open, and we were talking inside. Once he tied the animal in place, he activated the door. As it closed, he ran into the woods where he probably parked his car."

"But who's doing it, Phil, and why?"

"Probably the kid from the post. You went after him in the woods. Maybe you were getting close to something he's involved in, and he's telling you to back off."

She let out a deep breath. "I need to check out the area again tomorrow."

Phil held up a hand. "But not on your own. I'm going with you." He pulled out his cell. "And right now, we're calling the local police."

She started to object.

He shook his head. "They need to know what's going on."

"I can take care of myself, Phil."

"Of course you can, but this guy is turning into more than a vandal. The attacks against you and your property are becoming more assertive. The local cops need to know."

Of course Phil was right. Her own pride had kept her from calling before. She glanced once again at the dead animal. "Give me the phone. I'll make the call."

Officer Simpson was the same man she had spoken to yesterday. Once he arrived, Kelly explained everything that had happened, including the trap in the woods.

Mid-forties and competent, Simpson did a thorough search of the garage and surrounding area. Phil added an extra set of eyes, and Kelly remained vigilant for anything that might provide a clue as to why she was being harassed.

The officer took pictures of the possum before cutting down the animal. "Doubt we'll find anything on the carcass, but I'll have our people check it out. Sometimes we get lucky."

Kelly appreciated his thoroughness. While the death of a wild animal wasn't something the police normally worried about, the fact that the perpetrator was escalating his attacks was significant.

Simpson concluded with a warning. "You're going to have to be on your guard, ma'am. You're pretty far from town out here. Whoever's doing this has his sights on you. Keep that Sig Sauer of yours close at hand, and ensure your doors and windows remain locked. Might be good to have some floodlighting installed."

Phil cleared his throat and raised his brow.

She glanced at him and nodded. "That's what Captain Thibodeaux told me."

Phil stepped closer. "Let's deactivate this old automatic opener so it can't be triggered by any remote device. It'll mean you have to manually open and close the garage, Kelly, but that way you can keep the garage locked, which hopefully will deter anyone from entering again."

The cop nodded. "Good idea."

After disengaging the system, Phil manually lowered the door. "It'll take a bit of effort, but you'll be a lot safer. And when it's locked you'll know no one's getting inside."

"Thanks, Phil."

Turning back to the police officer, Kelly once again mentioned seeing Kyle Foglio in the woods and asked about the land that butted up to the Taylor farm.

"Sorry, I didn't get to it yet. I'll check it out in the morning. Might be a good idea if I send a squad car to examine those traps you mentioned. I'll call you first in case you want to meet me out there."

"I do." She pointed to Phil. "Would you have time to head back there tomorrow?"

Phil nodded. "Sounds like a good idea."

"I'll also want to see that trap you got caught in," the officer said to Kelly. He turned to Phil. "And those other ambushes you noticed."

"The one that snagged me has been disassembled," Kelly said. "As I mentioned, whoever is doing this left a portion of the rope in my car."

"Can your men be on the lookout for Kyle Foglio?" Phil asked.

The cop ran his hand over his chin and thought for a moment. "If the kid went to the high school in town, there would be a picture of him in the old yearbook. I'll copy the photo and circulate it through the department. We'll keep our eyes open and let you know if we spot him."

"As far as I know, he didn't stay in the area long, so he may not have had his photo taken at school, but it's worth a try," said Kelly. "I called the stepmother, but she didn't answer. Mrs. Foglio and Kyle didn't seem particularly close, but she might know something. I also called his real mom in Chicago. She didn't seem interested in her son or that he might have been injured."

"And the dad?" the cop asked.

"He's in jail."

Officer Simpson scratched his head. "You know what they say. The apple never falls far from the tree."

Phil was noticeably silent as the officer said good night and headed back to town.

"What's wrong?" Kelly asked, once they were alone.

"Maybe Kyle Foglio feels responsible for his dad going to prison."

"Why do you say that?"

He shrugged off the question and fumbled to offer an explanation about kids being easy to read. But as they walked back into her house, Kelly wondered if there wasn't something deeper that Phil was focused on, instead of a dead possum and a troubled teen.

The apple never falls far from the tree.

The cop's comment had hit Phil like a sucker punch to his gut. He'd heard that same comment whispered behind his back after his father had been arrested.

While helpful neighbors tried to contact his aunt, everyone wondered what would become of the little boy whose mother had abandoned him and whose father had been sent to jail.

Hard enough to be semi-orphaned. Even tougher to worry about growing up like the father he at one time had loved and admired.

In hindsight, the move to his aunt's house in DeRidder, Louisiana, a family-centered town with churches on every block, had been a positive influence on his young life. Aunt

Eleanor's deep conviction that the Lord was in control was a 180-degree flip from the absence of faith his folks had espoused. Even more significant had been her big heart for the child she had not borne and her innate ability to make Phil feel loved and accepted.

He had also been accepted by her church community. Many in the congregation were military families who became positive role models. His Scout leaders were commissioned officers and NCOs who taught him more about life and values and high moral standards than his dad had ever done in New Orleans.

The memories flashed through his mind before he had a chance to realize that Kelly seemed as despondent as he felt. Her arms were wrapped protectively around her waist, and she seemed unsure of what to do, now that they were both back in the kitchen. Recalling the tension-filled moment before the garage door had closed, Phil knew there was no going back in time.

Fate had undoubtedly saved him from making a fool of himself. If he had kissed Kelly—and that's exactly what he had wanted to do—the awkwardness of the current moment would be even more difficult.

"I should be leaving," he said as an opening, although he didn't want to leave her alone. "Sure you want to stay out here tonight? You could get a room at the Post Lodge. Might be a good option, at least for a few days."

"That would only mean that Kyle Foglio, or whoever is trying to frighten me, won. I'm staying put."

"You've got a stubborn streak, Kelly McQueen."

"Which is something my mother often reminded me of."

She stood looking at him expectantly, as if there was something else she was waiting for him to say. Finally she dropped her hands and sighed. "The cop's comment about the apple and the tree…"

He waited, wondering if she had checked into his own past and was going to bring up the painful events he kept buried. He had moved on from that time as a child. His dad had died shortly after his parole two years ago, and as far as Phil was concerned, that part of his life—the New Orleans days, as he often thought of them—was closed. He'd never gone back to the city and doubted he ever would.

"Well, I mean…" Kelly seemed to be having a hard time finding the right words. "I don't believe it, do you? It's just an old wives' tale, right?"

"It's merely a cliché, Kelly, that wagging tongues like to use to cause pain to anyone who has disappointed a parent."

"Sounds as if you speak from experience." The tilt of her head and her expressive eyes revealed a sadness he hadn't noticed earlier.

As openly expectant as she seemed, this wasn't the time to reveal his past. That part of his life was a closed door he refused to open.

"You need to expose the pain to the light, Philippe, in order to heal." Aunt Eleanor's words circled through his mind.

"Some doors should remain closed," he mumbled under his breath as he grabbed his hat.

Raising his voice, he added, "Keep your doors and windows locked as the cop instructed you, Kelly. Keep your cell phone turned on and at your bedside and make sure you've got the local police and my number programmed on speed dial."

A small but refreshing smile cracked her lips and brought a bit of lightness to the weight she had carried on her shoulders just moments before.

"Call that garage repairman in the morning and find out why he stood you up. Also, get a good electrician out here to install floods in the rear of your property." He glanced at her front door. "Dead bolts would be good, as well."

"Phil, I've got to be on post bright and early. We've got an ongoing investigation."

"Which I'm well aware of."

She lowered her gaze. "Sorry. Of course you are. I'll be fine tonight."

She took a step toward the door and grimaced.

"That leg's still bothering you?"

"Only occasionally."

"Use an ice pack, keep it elevated and think about going on sick call in the morning."

"Yes, sir." She smiled and gave him a semi-salute.

He shook his head but couldn't hide the smile on his lips. "You are one stubborn woman."

"I believe you just said that."

He opened the door and turned to look at her. She stepped closer, and for an instant, he wanted to kiss her as he had wanted to do earlier in the kitchen.

"Thanks for the pizza," she said, dispelling the moment.

"Yeah." He slapped his hat against his leg. "Lock the door and call me if you need me."

Once he got to his truck, he turned to stare back at her house, doubtful Kelly McQueen would ever need him, and that realization made the night seem even colder.

TEN

Phil had a mountain of paperwork to review the next day as well as a company of men who needed to be assured that they hadn't done anything wrong. At least that's what Phil believed and would continue to believe until evidence—cold, hard evidence—came to light.

Even the first sergeant, a battle-worn veteran who usually rolled with the punches, was concerned about the company.

"Sir, this whole situation has my gut in turmoil. I talked to Staff Sergeant Gates after PT this morning. He was telling me about Taylor's squad and how the death is affecting the men. Guess Stanley had another hard night. A number of the guys stayed up trying to reassure him." The first sergeant rubbed his short hair. "Have to tell you, I can relate. Even my wife and daughter, Marie, say I'm not myself."

"You're not the only one." Phil let out a deep breath in hopes of easing the tension that tightened his shoulders.

Riffling through the files on his desk, Phil asked, "Did the protocol office send over the list of people who were invited to attend the live-fire event?"

"Not yet, sir. I'll see if I can get the list for you." Meyers left Phil's office in haste, no doubt happy to have a reason to head back to his desk.

Kelly continued to interview the men and had a thick

notebook of statements she wanted to discuss with Phil. Not that he minded. Having someone outside the unit to discuss the incident with was helpful, especially when she brought in hoagie sandwiches for lunch and a bag of chocolate chip cookies she'd picked up at the commissary.

They ate on paper plates and drank another pot of coffee until her phone rang. She dropped the notes they had been reviewing and pulled her cell to her ear.

"Officer Simpson, thanks for calling me back." She listened for a moment and then nodded. "That sounds good, but let me check with Captain Thibodeaux."

Covering the phone with her hand, she glanced at Phil. "Simpson's heading out to the trailer site. He said he'd meet us there."

Phil nodded. "Let's do it."

"We'll be there shortly," she told Simpson.

A squad car sat parked beside the trailer as Phil pulled his pickup into the clearing. Simpson and a second police officer, in his mid-twenties with blond hair and a slender build, stepped out of the trailer as Phil and Kelly pulled to a stop.

"I got a court order to search the premises." Simpson held up a plastic evidence bag containing the bloodstained shirt. "We'll test the stains and see what we come up with."

After placing the evidence in his car, he motioned them toward the woods. "Let's take a look at those traps."

They fanned out, covered a large area in a short period of time and found three traps rigged exactly like the one that had caught Kelly.

"They remind me of what we did in Ranger School," Phil said after examining the last of the snares. "Of course, we were hoping to catch rabbit to eat and not anything larger."

Simpson nodded. "I noticed the Ranger tab on your shoulder, Captain. Have to admire anyone who goes through that grueling ordeal. Pure misery, the way I hear tell."

Kelly's lips twitched. She evidently enjoyed seeing him squirm under Officer Simpson's praise. Surely she realized Phil hadn't mentioned Ranger School to spotlight his own accomplishments.

Hoping to deflect attention off himself, Phil said, "The traps were set in a line between the road and the makeshift campsite."

Simpson rubbed his jaw. "Probably to deter folks from making it to the clearing. The rope looks weatherworn. My guess, the traps were set a few years back."

The younger officer's brow wrinkled. "But why would anyone go to all that trouble, when there's a back road that runs the length of the property on the far side of the clearing?"

Simpson nodded. "Good point, but how many folks know about that old path?"

The younger officer smiled. "Only the high school kids who park out there, and the cops who patrol the area."

Kelly put her hands on her hips. "So Kyle Foglio could have known about another road?"

"Could be." Simpson checked his watch. "Hate to cut this short, but it looks like we've found what we came out here for and I need to be at police headquarters."

He led the way back to the squad car and pointed to a thick wooded area on the far side of the cleaning. "That path runs north and south over in that area. You can pick it up just beyond the intersection of Hastings Road and State Road 15."

"By the small Stop and Shop?" Phil asked.

"About two hundred yards west of there. Probably hard to find at night. I'd scout it out in daylight, if I were you."

Kelly glanced at Phil. "We could drive by the turnoff on our way back to post."

Phil nodded as he opened the passenger door for her. "I've

got time, if you do." She thanked Simpson and the other officer before she climbed into the pickup.

Stepping away from his truck, Phil lowered his voice so only Simpson would hear. "I'd appreciate it if you could keep an eye out for that Foglio kid. Agent McQueen underplays the significance of the garage breakins, but they have me worried."

"You and I are thinking alike, Captain."

Phil handed him his business card. "Let me know if you find the kid."

"Will do."

"What was that about?" Kelly asked when he climbed behind the wheel.

"Nothing important."

She raised her brow and eyed him with suspicion, but he refused to divulge anything more.

Kelly watched the two police officers head back to town as Phil turned onto State Road 15 and searched for the turn-off into the woods. The entrance was overgrown, and if Simpson hadn't told them, they never would have realized the dirt road existed.

"Let's see how far north it runs," Kelly suggested.

"Looks like someone's been this way recently," Phil said, pointing to tire tracks.

Kelly stared into the distance as they passed the trailer and continued north. Leaves had fallen from the trees, which improved visibility. She put her hand on Phil's arm. "Pull up here."

He did as she asked and followed her gaze. "Well, how about that."

From where they parked, the outline of a farmhouse could be seen on the far side of the trees. "The Taylor farm," Kelly said. "Interesting that the two properties are connected by the dirt road."

As they watched, Lola stepped outside and hastened to the cages by the woodpile in her backyard, not far from the old barn.

"Can you make out what she's doing?" Kelly asked.

Phil opened his glove compartment. Pulling out a pair of binoculars, he handed them to her. "See if these help."

Kelly lifted the glasses to her eyes and adjusted the focus. "She's feeding the roosters she said would be picked up last night. Although she's glancing around as if she's worried someone will see her."

Once Lola went back into the house, Phil turned the truck around. They passed the clearing where the trailer was parked, keeping their eyes peeled for any sign of a teenage boy.

Seeing nothing out of the ordinary, Phil smiled at Kelly. He started to say something just as a gunshot rang out.

She looked out the back window. "Did you hear that?"

"Sounded like a rifle."

A second round exploded, shattering the truck's rear tail-light.

Phil's face tightened. He tramped down on the accelerator. "Get down, Kelly."

She placed her hand on the dash for support and ducked her head. The truck bounced over the rough terrain.

Peering out the passenger window at the side mirror, Kelly scanned the forest and dense underbrush behind them for any sign of movement. "I don't see anyone."

Phil flicked his gaze between the two side mirrors. "Neither do I, but someone's out there."

A third shot.

Kelly flinched. Her heartbeat accelerated.

"Stay low." Phil gripped the wheel and steered around the ruts in the narrow path.

The main road was just ahead. Turning onto the hardtop, he gunned the engine, leaving a streak of black on the pavement.

Rising in the seat, Kelly let out a deep breath. "Not my favorite way to spend the afternoon."

"Are you all right?"

"Just concerned. That couldn't have been a hunter."

"Not unless his aim was way off."

"I'll call Simpson." She reached for her cell, and once the police officer answered, Kelly quickly explained what happened.

"He's sending two squad cars to check out the area," she told Phil after she disconnected. Seconds later, the sound of sirens filled the air.

Although the danger had passed, the realization of what had happened settled over Kelly. Had the shots been a warning or a blatant attempt to do them harm?

Phil eased up on the accelerator and pulled into a deserted gas station. Glancing over their shoulders, they watched the police cars approach from the opposite direction and turn onto the dirt path.

Stepping to the pavement, Phil rounded his truck and examined the broken taillight. Kelly joined him there.

"Sorry about the damage," she said.

"The light can be fixed." Looking down at her, he felt a sense of relief. "At least neither of us was hurt."

"Do you think it was a warning not to snoop around the trailer?"

Phil shrugged. "I'm not sure. But I'd like to head north on the Freemont Road and check out the Taylor place."

"In case Lola saw something?"

"Or someone. Remember how she seemed on edge when she was feeding the roosters?"

"But would she admit it, Phil, if she had seen something?"

"Maybe not verbally, but her body language might be more revealing."

Kelly titled her head. "So we show up on her doorstep and ask if she heard gunfire?"

Phil patted the pocket of his uniform and smiled. "The men took up a collection to help with the funeral expenses. I need to give her the money. We can start on that note and then mention the shots."

"I'll follow your lead." Once they climbed back into the truck, Kelly asked, "Has the survival assistance officer talked to her yet?"

"He met with her this morning. The insurance forms have been submitted, but they'll take time to process. If she's like the majority of military families, she'll have bills to pay before the check arrives."

Kelly buckled her seat belt. "It's nice of the men to donate."

Phil nodded as he pulled back onto the road. "Chaplain Sanchez encouraged them to dig deep. He said if the tables were turned, they'd want their own families supported."

"For being new to the army, the chaplain's not afraid to get involved."

"He's been an asset to Lieutenant Bellows. The chaplain has been visiting the men and ensuring they've got his ear when they need to talk."

"How's Private Stanley?" she asked.

"Better. Sanchez asked some of the other men in the platoon to include the kid whenever they do anything. He said it's starting to pay off."

At the intersection of Freemont Road, Phil turned north. "You locked your doors this morning, didn't you?"

"And the garage. I shouldn't have any more problems."

"What about the repairman who stood you up yesterday?" Phil asked.

"His child got sick, and he had to pick her up from day care. Evidently, she had a temperature and needed to go to the doctor. He said he would have called me, but he left my number at his shop."

"Did you set up another appointment?"

Kelly nodded. "He's booked for the rest of the week, but we've tentatively set a date for Monday, as long as I can leave work early that day."

"Which means you'll have to manually raise and lower your garage door for the rest of the week."

She smiled. "It's okay, Phil."

He glanced at her leg. "And your ankle?"

"Feeling much better, thank you for asking."

Phil turned his gaze back to the road and forest beyond. Although he thought the shooter was probably long gone, he needed to be careful, especially with Kelly onboard.

As they rounded the final curve, he put on the turn signal, pulled into the Taylor driveway and parked next to the house. After giving the area a visual sweep, he climbed out. "Maybe you should stay in the truck."

Kelly shook her head and stepped down onto the gravel drive. "No way. We're in this together."

"Haven't we discussed your stubbornness?"

She raised her brow. "As if you aren't the same."

They were both smiling as they climbed the porch steps, but when Phil rapped on the door, no one answered.

"I'm worried about Mildred." Kelly glanced around. "Lola planned to tell her about her son's death. The news would have been a blow. Maybe she needed medical care."

Phil peered into one of the windows. "I can't see anything. The curtains are pulled together tight."

"Let's circle around to the back of the house and check Mildred's bedroom."

Walking in front of Kelly, Phil scanned the area around the house as well as the surrounding woods. He paused for a moment at the side of the structure, listening.

Finally, he nodded for Kelly to follow him. "Stay behind me," he cautioned.

She tugged on his arm. "In case you forgot, I'm the cop with the gun."

He almost smiled again. "Yeah, but a gentlemen always protects a lady."

Kelly tilted her head. "Aunt Eleanor?"

"Exactly. She told me ladies go first, except if there's danger." He winked. "Then the man takes the lead."

Stretching, Phil tried to look into the rear windows, but they were too far off the ground, and the drapes were drawn, as well.

Cautiously, he approached the back door and pounded his knuckles against the sturdy oak. When no one answered, he glanced over his shoulder to the barn. "You wait here. I want to get a look at those roosters."

"I'll go with you."

Phil's reflexes were on high alert as they walked across the backyard to where the birds were caged. Two were white with long tail feathers. The others were a rusty red. Each bird eyed them warily.

Phil stooped down to get a closer look. "Check out the talon on the big one with red feathers. Something's on his leg."

Kelly bent lower. "Could it be tape?"

Phil opened the cage and grabbed the bird with two hands, immobilizing its wings. "See if you can pull it off."

Kelly grasped the bird's leg and used her fingernail to remove the green tape, which she held out to Phil as he placed the bird back in the cage. "Army issue duct tape. But why would it be around the bird's leg?"

"It could have held a small knife, called a gaff, in place. People remove the natural spurs on the roosters and attach the razor-sharp gaffs, which can be deadly when they attack. Handlers often feed drugs to the roosters to make them mean. They're bred to fight to the death, although the battles are so bloody that often both birds die in the fights."

Kelly shook her head. "What a horrid sport, if you could even call it that."

"Which includes big-stakes gambling. Both the cockfights and the betting are outlawed in most states." Phil brushed his hands off and pointed into the barn. "I wonder if Lola is planning a trip."

Kelly followed his gaze and saw the travel trailer parked in the barn. Phil looked around nervously. "Let's get out of here. I've got a strange feeling someone may be watching us."

Kelly glanced over her shoulder. "You think it might be the person who fired those shots earlier?"

"I have no idea, but I believe what my body is telling me. Right now it's saying, 'Get in your pickup truck and drive away.'"

ELEVEN

Phil steered his truck south along the Freemont Road while he tried to put the pieces of the strange puzzle together. Who had shot at them and why? A large area beyond the Taylor farm and neighboring property was rife with game, but even the worst of shots wouldn't have mistaken his truck for wildlife.

Kelly had mentioned a warning. Perhaps to stay away from the clearing and the trailer? In Phil's opinion, Kyle Foglio was probably the marksman, which made Phil even more concerned about Kelly's safety.

The traps in the woods were a concern, as well. They had military written all over them, but a soldier didn't have to have a Ranger tab on his shoulder to know how to build a snare.

Had their purpose been to keep folks from wandering off the road and into the clearing by the old deserted trailer? And if so, then why? Did the caged gamecocks somehow play into the mystery, as well?

Kelly tilted her head in his direction. "I'm concerned about what Lola might be involved in, Phil, especially after seeing the birds up close."

"I was thinking the same thing," he admitted. "Yet we

could be jumping to the wrong conclusions. The roosters might belong to a friend of hers, just as she claimed."

"She said the owner planned to pick them up."

Phil nodded. "But plans change. The friend could still be out of town."

"I'm worried about Mildred."

Although he didn't want to alarm Kelly, he was concerned, as well. "If she needed medical care, where would Lola take her?"

Kelly thought for a moment. "There's a hospital in town, but Lola mentioned taking Mildred to a geriatric clinic. I saw a medicine bottle in her drawer. The prescribing doctor's name was Kutter, and the Kutter Geriatric Clinic Pharmacy filled the prescription. Have you heard of it?"

"No, but there's a place close by where we might be able to learn more about the doc and his clinic."

Kelly's brow wrinkled. "I'm not following you."

"Magnolia Gardens. Surely you know a nurse or two who could direct us. If the Kutter Clinic isn't too far from here, we might be able check on Mildred before we head back to post."

Kelly grabbed at a lock of her hair. "I'm not sure I feel up to visiting the home, Phil."

Her comment surprised him. Usually Kelly was eager to follow up on any clue or bit of information.

"Because of your mom?" he asked.

She let out a deep sigh. "It's probably silly of me, but I haven't visited Magnolia Gardens since the night my mother died. I… I'm not sure I can handle going back."

"The grieving process is a tough battle to fight, Kelly, especially if you try to do it alone."

She bit her lip and looked more like a timid child than a CID agent. "But—" Her voice was not much more than a whisper. "You're probably right about the nurses being able to locate Mildred's doctor."

"Someone may even remember her. Didn't Lola say her mother-in-law had been in the home?"

Kelly seemed to take heart at Phil's last comment. "Which means we might be able to track Mildred down after all."

Magnolia Gardens appeared in the distance. Phil lowered his speed and pulled into the parking lot. When he opened the passenger door, Kelly hesitated before climbing out.

He reached for her hand. "We'll go inside together. If it becomes too much for you, let me know, and we can leave."

She gave him a weak smile and slipped her hand into his. The put-together CID agent had exposed a little of her own vulnerability. Kelly's mother was gone, so she turned her attention and a portion of her heart to Mildred. No doubt it was easier to worry about the very-much-alive Senior Mrs. Taylor than to wallow in grief for her own mother who had passed on.

Hand in hand, Phil and Kelly walked toward the main door of the healthcare facility. *Give her the comfort she needs now, Lord,* Phil prayed. Then he stopped short, realizing what he had just done.

After all these years of denying the existence of a loving God, Phil had just uttered a prayer, brief through it was, to help Kelly.

He glanced down at her. Was she a good influence on him? Or was he going off in a direction he would soon regret?

Déjà vu, Kelly thought as she entered the nursing home with Phil. Once again he was supporting her, just as he'd done the night she had been caught in the trap. She wouldn't have had the courage to come back to Magnolia Gardens if he hadn't promised to be at her side.

Phil glanced down the long hallway and squeezed her hand. "Which way?"

"My...my mother's room was to the left. The nurses' station is not far beyond her room. I should be able to ask one of the nurses on duty about Mildred."

Pulling in a deep breath, Kelly turned down the hallway she had walked so many times before. Every night for a whole year she had stopped by to see her mom.

"My mother eventually got so weak," Kelly told Phil. "I tried to get here in time to feed her."

"Which she appreciated, I'm sure."

Kelly didn't say anything to the contrary. Instead she thought about the routine into which she and her mother had fallen. A routine that left neither of them interested in getting to the bottom of the main issue that stood between them. Ignoring the problem was easier than giving voice to the pain of the past that each woman preferred to leave buried.

Now that her mother was gone, Kelly knew they should have brought that deep-seated pain to the surface. Although, Kelly couldn't have stood more condemnation. Once upon a time, she had heaped enough on her own shoulders.

She'd worked through most of the guilt and her own self-doubt. At least, she told herself she had. Although now, returning to Magnolia Gardens, she knew there were issues deep within her that still needed to heal.

"My mother's room is just around the corner." Kelly clutched Phil's arm, unable to remember the last time she had felt so needy. She had handled the paperwork and burial arrangements by herself and had remained strong throughout the funeral. Today, the pain of losing her mother seemed so raw.

A gray-haired woman in a wheelchair sat in the doorway of her mother's room. Recognizing Kelly, her mocha face opened with a wide smile. "Sure is good to see you again, sugar."

"Mrs. Baker, how are you?"

"Fair to middling. You know what I always tell the good Lord. I'm ready whenever He is. So far, He keeps saying I'm needed here."

Tears burned Kelly's eyes as she released hold of Phil's hand and bent down to hug the sweet older lady. The woman pulled her close and patted her shoulders as if she was a babe needing to be soothed.

Kelly stepped back and, once again, took Phil's hand. "Mrs. Baker, I want to introduce my friend, Captain Jean Philippe Thibodeaux."

His smile matched the woman's. "A pleasure, ma'am."

"Nice to meet such a fine-looking soldier." Her eyes twinkled as she glanced from Phil to Kelly. "Your mama would be so happy about you having a boyfriend."

"Oh, Mrs. Baker." Kelly started to object. "Phil and I are—"

The woman continued to talk as if she hadn't heard Kelly's protest. "Your mama was worried about you, honey child. Being alone and all. She said the military wasn't a good life for her daughter."

Kelly bit her lip. Her mother hadn't approved of much of what she had done, but she didn't want to deter Mrs. Baker. The woman had a heart as big as the sky, and Kelly enjoyed basking in the love that seemed to flow out to all those around her.

Mrs. Baker smiled up at Phil and grabbed his free hand. "You've got a jewel here with Kelly."

"Yes, ma'am, I'm well aware of how special she is."

He glanced at Kelly over Mrs. Baker's head, causing Kelly's cheeks to heat. She tilted her head and rolled her eyes, trying to signal that Mrs. Baker often jumped to the wrong conclusions, which she was doing at the present time.

His smile remained in place, and he seemed totally engaged with the older woman. "Now, Mrs. Baker, you know a lot of young men are interested in Kelly, so I feel extremely blessed that she singled me out."

"Uh-huh. You're right about the other men. Mrs. Walker in room 205 has a son who asked Kelly out more than once, but she always turned him down."

"She was saving her love for me." Phil winked at the sweet woman.

"She sure was, Jean Philippe. Looks like she found herself a good man, for sure. But I need you to promise me something."

Phil raised his brow. "What's that, ma'am?"

"That you'll take good care of my Kelly."

"Yes, ma'am. I promise." He glanced at Kelly and his smile made her cheeks burn. "Cross my heart."

Not wanting to encourage Mrs. Baker any more and hoping to keep Phil from embarrassing himself and her as well, Kelly turned her back on the two of them and glanced into the small double bedroom.

A new resident rested on the bed her mother had previously occupied. The plump woman with full cheeks and an equally wide smile raised her head from the pillow and waved a greeting, which Kelly instantly returned, feeling a sense of relief.

She had been so worried about how she would handle seeing her mother's empty bed, but the new resident and her friendly smile drove home the point that life went on.

Kelly turned back to Mrs. Baker. "Is Grace on duty this afternoon?"

"She sure is. I saw her a few minutes ago and asked her to bring me some ice cream."

"I'll get it for you." Kelly reached for Phil's arm. "Why don't you come with me, Captain. We'll find the nurse and Mrs. Baker's ice cream."

"But we were enjoying our conversation." He waved jovially at the older woman as Kelly pulled him away.

Kelly pretended annoyance as she ushered him toward the nurses' station. "Do you attract women wherever you go?"

"It's the Cajun charm, *ma chère.*" His eyes twinkled and the rich sound of his laughter filled the hallway. She laughed, too, which surprised her almost as much as her lifted spirits.

"Mrs. Baker likes strawberry ice cream, which you'll find in the freezer in that room." Kelly pointed to a small utility closet. "I'll locate Grace, if you would be kind enough to take Mrs. Baker her snack. Spoons are beside the refrigerator."

"Yes, ma'am." As he headed off, Kelly called after him. "But don't stay too long with Mrs. Baker. We need to talk to the nurse." Phil raised his hand in agreement before he stepped toward the freezer.

Kelly found the nurse at the far end of the hallway. Grace, a tall woman with a big heart, opened her arms and wrapped Kelly in a welcoming embrace. Once again, Kelly felt acceptance and support. Grace had cared for her mother and had loved her as much as Kelly did.

"I should have stopped by before now. You were so good to Mom."

Grace kept one arm around Kelly's shoulder as they walked back to the nurses' station. "I know how hard it is to come back. Lots of family members say they will visit. Few actually do. The memories are just too painful."

Kelly nodded. "That's how I felt, but seeing the new resident in Mom's room had the opposite effect on me."

The nurse squeezed Kelly's shoulder. "I'm glad. Mrs. Peters moved here from Augusta to be close to her children."

"Like my mother had to move to be with me."

"It happens often, Kelly. You were very attentive to her needs. She often told me how lucky she was to have such a wonderful daughter."

Kelly stopped and stared at the nurse. "Are you sure you're not thinking of Mrs. Baker?"

"Although Mrs. Baker says the same thing about her children, I certainly remember your mother on more than one occasion mentioning her love for you."

The nurse's comment was like a stab to Kelly heart. She couldn't determine if it was pain or relief that brought tears to her eyes.

Hearing footsteps, she turned to find Phil staring at her. Understanding was clearly written on his face. Swiping her hand across her cheeks, she introduced him to Grace before explaining they needed to ask her a few questions.

The nurse guided them into a small side room and invited them both to take a seat around the conference table. "Would you like some coffee?"

"No, thanks. We'll only keep you for a minute." Kelly hoped the nurse would provide the answers they needed. "I'm trying to locate Kutter Geriatric Clinic in one of the surrounding towns. The physician's name is Addison Kutter."

The nurse hesitated for a moment, her gaze going between Kelly and Phil. "It's in Carmichael. About an hour-and-a-half drive from here."

Kelly's spirits sagged as she looked at Phil. "That's too far for us to go this afternoon and a long distance for an older person to travel to see a doctor. Do you have their phone number?" Grace wrote it on a piece of paper and handed it to Kelly.

Then the nurse folded her hands on the table and looked a bit uncomfortable. "I probably shouldn't say anything, but rumors have been floating around."

"About the clinic?"

Grace took a deep breath. "And about Dr. Addison Kutter who owns the place. Evidently a whistle-blower came forward."

"Someone who works for him?"

The nurse nodded. "His treatments have been questioned by a number of leading physicians in the state. I heard recently his records are being reviewed for ethical standards violations."

"Meaning what?" Kelly asked.

"From what I've heard, the doctor is heavy-handed with his medication protocols."

"So he overprescribes?"

Grace shrugged. "Let's just say he's aggressive."

"The woman I'm concerned about suffers from osteoarthritis and dementia and may have some problem regulating her blood sugar. Kutter prescribed oxycodone, 80 milligrams."

"She may need it for her pain, but I wouldn't want him treating anyone I knew, that's for sure."

Kelly scooted to the edge of her chair. "Do you remember a resident named Mildred Taylor?"

"When was she here?"

"A year ago," Kelly answered. Then she added, "But you started working at Magnolia Gardens after my mother moved in."

"That's right. I've had this job for ten months, so I wouldn't have known Mildred, but Sally Jacobs might. She's been here for over five years and is working tomorrow. I can ask her if she remembers Mildred."

"That would help." Kelly pulled her business card from her pocket and gave it to the nurse. "You can reach me on my cell phone."

"I'll let you know what Sally says." Grace glanced at her watch. "It's time for me to distribute the meds, so I'd better get going. Both of you need to come back and see us again."

Kelly promised they would.

Mrs. Baker was still in the hallway when they walked by her room. After giving her a parting hug, Kelly happened to ask, "Mrs. Baker, do you remember a resident named Mildred Taylor?"

The old woman shook her head. "Don't recall anyone name Mildred. 'Course there was a Millie Taylor."

Kelly's pulse quickened. "Did she move out about a year ago?"

Ms. Baker pursed her full lips. "Seems about right. She said she was going to be with her son. Millie was cute as a pie. She could walk. Why, she'd do laps around the other residents. All of us were real happy that she was doing so good and could go home."

The old woman glanced at Phil. "That's what everyone wants, you know."

"I know it's hard to leave your home." Kelly patted Mrs. Baker's hand before she asked, "Do you remember if Millie's son was in the army?"

The old woman nodded. "He had been in Kentucky, but the army moved him down here. Made Millie real happy."

"I'm sure it did." A strange feeling swept over Kelly. "Now that you mention it, I seem to remember hearing about Millie."

Mrs. Baker smiled knowingly. "Why sure, honey child. Your mama moved in a day or two after Millie left. Don't you remember me telling you about Millie Taylor? She was my old roommate. Your mama got her bed."

TWELVE

As Phil drove them back to post, Kelly called Dr. Kutter's clinic and inquired about Mildred Taylor. No one by that name had been admitted into the short-term care center or to the Freemont Hospital when she called that facility.

Her third call was to the Labor Department's office in Atlanta that handled Medicare fraud in Georgia. Although the agent with whom she spoke couldn't reveal specific information, he did indicate there was some question about Dr. Kutter's practice.

Ironic though it was that Mildred Taylor had left Magnolia Gardens at the time when Kelly needed to find a bed for her own mother, Phil wondered if releasing Millie to Lola's care had been in the older woman's best interest. He was beginning to agree with Kelly that the daughter-in-law's actions seemed questionable.

Once they were in his office, Kelly threw her hands in the air, needing to vent some of her frustration. "Mrs. Baker said Mildred was walking and physically fit when she left the home. Now's she's bedridden and senile."

Although Kelly echoed his own concerns, Phil did offer an explanation. "A year can be a long time for someone her age."

"Yes, but—"

The chirp of Kelly's cell phone interrupted her reply. "This is Special Agent McQueen." She glanced down. "That's right."

The intense look on Kelly's face indicated the call was important. Phil watched as she focused her attention on the person on the other end of the line.

"Thanks for rushing the ballistic tests through."

Phil's gut tightened. He pulled in a deep breath, wondering what the Atlanta CID lab had determined.

Kelly nodded. "Right." She made a notation on a tablet she pulled from her purse.

"You're sure?" Another pause. "Thanks."

She hung up and looked at Phil. "The CID ballistic testing lab got a match."

Drawing a second notebook from her purse, she rifled through the pages. "Here it is. The weapon was issued to—"

She glanced up at Phil, her eyes wide. "This is interesting. The round that killed Corporal Taylor was fired from Private Benjamin Stanley's M-4 carbine."

"Are you sure?"

"The lab techs said it was a good match."

Phil walked around his desk. "And Stanley is a good soldier."

"Who's had the hardest time dealing with Taylor's death." She reached for her purse. "I need to talk to Stanley. Would you call Lieutenant Bellows and tell him I'm coming over to the platoon headquarters? See if he can round up the private."

Phil grabbed his hat. "You're not going alone. I want to talk to him, as well."

As they left Phil's office and headed across the grassy knoll to the platoon area, he turned to Kelly. "How do you plan to handle this?"

"Very carefully. You realize this man more than likely

killed another solider. Trust me, Phil, I'm not going to do anything you wouldn't approve."

"I'm concerned about Stanley."

"I'm more concerned about Corporal Taylor. He deserves to have the truth revealed about his death and his killer."

"You mean the man who accidentally fired the fatal round," Phil corrected.

"Okay, I need to watch my words, but let me do my job."

Phil narrowed his eyes, frustrated by the direction of their conversation. "As if I'm not?"

"You're getting emotional."

"Kelly, this happens to be my company."

"Which many of the men think you lead with an iron hand."

"Meaning?"

"They said you shouldn't have held the live-fire exercise after four nights in the field. Everyone was tired. Dead tired, a number of them said."

"We were in the field for four days, and yes, some of the men failed to get much sleep, but they're young and healthy. You know I couldn't do something that wasn't approved by the battalion commander."

"Who seems to cut you a lot of slack. I'm not saying you did anything wrong, Phil, but fatigue may have played into Taylor's death."

"The men will thank me the next time they head for combat. Some of them joined the company in the past month. If they're not adequately trained, they might not know how to respond in a deployment. I'm not doing the training just to keep the brass happy. You understand that, don't you, Kelly?

Her voice softened. "Would it make any difference if I said I did?"

"It would make me feel as if at least one person is on my side."

"I am, Phil. But I'm also on the side of justice, which is what we're both after."

"I'm after answers."

"And justice," she prodded.

He shrugged. "And justice. But I want to get to the bottom of what happened."

"As do I. I've been assigned to investigate Taylor's death. My boss and your boss and the commanding general expect answers, which I will provide."

"You don't understand. This is personal to me. Not because of what people will think or any efficiency report I might get or reprimand, if you find that I was at fault, but because I won't continue on as an army officer if something I did wrong caused Taylor's death."

"Mistakes happen, Phil. That's what this investigation is about. If there was a safety issue that wasn't addressed and should have been then changes will be made. If the blame falls on your shoulders, you go on. You don't walk away."

"How would you know?"

"Because I made a mistake years ago. I was only fifteen. It haunts me to this day, but I can't let what happened hold me back or stop me from doing my job."

"Whatever mistake you made had nothing to do with completing a mission. If I lost a man in a noncombat situation, there's no way I could feel competent leading in combat."

She shook her head and pursed her lips as she glared up at him. Lines of frustration twisted her face. "Pride."

"What?"

"You heard me. You've got a problem with pride. You think you're too good to make a mistake, and if anyone says you did do something that led to Taylor's death then you could never forgive yourself, nor ask forgiveness from your commanders."

"My superiors won't be the problem. It's the soldiers. How

will I ask their forgiveness? The men have to have complete confidence in their commander's ability." He jammed his thumb back at his chest. "In my ability."

"They know you're human. You're not giving them enough credit."

Kelly handled situations after the fact. Easy enough to be a Saturday-morning quarterback, which is what her work involved. Someone messes up, and the CID was called in to investigate and point the blame. But she had never been the one who had to make a decision in combat that could cause loss of life.

As much as he was starting to like Kelly, her focus was completely the opposite of his. Plus, she was focused on her job and the answers she needed. Why would he even think that she would understand his side of the situation?

He pointed to the platoon headquarters. "Let's get this done, and then we can discuss where we go next."

"Where we go?" She stared up at him, and for a brief second, they both realized there was more in that one phrase than just the investigation.

As if on cue, they turned toward the small brick building where Stanley would be waiting for them, knowing full well that there were other issues between them that had started to surface.

Phil needed to detach himself from the feelings he had for Kelly and focus instead on the investigation. He didn't need her support or her friendship, and yet those were the only things that made sense at the present moment.

The atmosphere in the platoon headquarters was heavy enough to cut with a bayonet. Lieutenant Bellows and squad leader Sergeant Gates had long faces and their eyes reflected the dark mood that Kelly sensed from Phil. The company commander had been brutally honest about what was on the line for him personally. She'd bet the lieutenant felt the same way.

No one had mentioned the ballistics test to Stanley who probably wondered why he had been summoned. Kelly planned to break the ice with the private with a few questions and then take him back verbally to the live fire and see what his memory revealed. She had a transcript of their original interview, which she would compare with what the soldier had to say today. Any deviation would be noted. Body language would play heavily into it.

Plus, her sixth sense, that innate ability to read people, would have a bearing, as well. Although she wouldn't mention it to Phil. He wanted everything cut-and-dried and able to be seen and discerned on a very rational basis.

She pulled in a breath and nodded to the lieutenant and Staff Sergeant Gates. Both men stood as she and Phil entered the platoon leader's office. Gates was a big, muscular guy who was as tall as the lieutenant but twice as broad.

"Ma'am, I've got Private Stanley in a side office," Lieutenant Bellows said. "You'll be able to talk to him there. He's a good soldier who does a good job most days. I find it hard to believe that he—"

She held up her hand. To his credit, Bellows dropped the comment and nodded. "It's your call, isn't it, ma'am?"

"Exactly." She glanced at Phil. "The captain and I will need complete privacy while we discuss the incident with Private Stanley."

"Of course."

"Who else knows what ballistics uncovered?"

"We're the only two in the platoon, ma'am. The captain said to keep the information close-hold."

She nodded. "Good."

Kelly and Phil walked to the small room where Private

Stanley sat at one side of a metal table. His hands were in his lap and his legs crossed at his ankles.

Seeing them enter, he leapt to his feet and saluted. "Sir. Ma'am."

"At ease, Private." Phil closed the door as Kelly chose a chair across from Stanley. Phil lowered himself into the seat to her right.

The soldier was young, probably nineteen or twenty, with a round face and big eyes that stared at Kelly from across the table. "Lieutenant Bellows said you wanted to talk to me, ma'am."

"That's right." She placed a folder on the table and looked at Stanley for a long moment before she spoke. "You know I'm with the CID on post and am investigating Corporal Taylor's death."

Stanley nodded. "Yes, ma'am. You talked to me the night Rick died."

"That's correct." Kelly opened the folder. "You were issued a weapon—an M-4 carbine—before the live-fire exercise." Glancing at her notes, she read off the serial number. "Is that your weapon?"

"Yes, ma'am. But actually I checked it out of the arms room before we went to the field. Just like the other men did. That was four days before live fire."

"Did you keep your weapon with you at all times, Private?"

He glanced up at the ceiling as if reflecting on all that had happened. "I can't think of any time that it was out of my sight, ma'am."

"And that would include throughout the training exercise?"

"If you mean live fire, then yes, ma'am. I kept my weapon on my person just as I'm supposed to do."

"Did you put it down or leave it unattended at any time?" Kelly pressed.

Again, he paused. "Only when Corporal Ramsey stumbled."

Kelly raised her brow ever so slightly and glanced at Phil. His expression never changed, but she noted the tension in his jaw as he scooted closer to the table.

"What happened to Corporal Ramsey?"

"I'm not sure, sir. It was getting dark. The ground was uneven in that area. Later, Ramsey told me he hadn't gotten much sleep in the field."

Phil's hands fisted. "None of the men had, Stanley."

"You're right about that, sir. Not that I'm complaining. I learn a lot every time we go out to the field. The way I see it, sir, you're helping me get ready for when I have to deploy."

"Hopefully the unit will be stateside for a period of time."

"But we need to be ready, sir."

Kelly turned the questioning back to live fire. "When you helped Corporal Ramsey, what did you do with your rifle?"

"Ah—" The soldier hesitated. "I handed it off."

"To whom?"

"Well, ma'am." Stanley bit his lower lip. "I've been trying to think who it could have been. For the life of me, I can't remember."

Kelly glanced at the notes she'd taken the night of the incident. "You didn't mention leaving your rifle the first time we talked."

"No, ma'am."

When the soldier didn't provide a reason, Phil asked, "How long was the weapon out of your sight?"

The troop shrugged. "Not long, sir. Maybe a minute or so. Long enough for Ramsey to get his bearings. Then I hurried back to the old tree stump to retrieve the rifle."

Phil raised his brow. "I thought you said you handed the M-4 to someone?"

"I did, sir. But I was next to the tree stump at the time. When I returned, my weapon was resting against the stump."

Kelly folded her hands and leaned forward. "A lot was happening. The confusion of the battlefield could have thrown you off. Perhaps you thought you were passing off your M-4, when in reality you dropped the weapon."

Stanley scratched his jaw. "That seems unlikely, ma'am."

"Oh?" Kelly waited for an explanation.

"Because I remember passing the gun *into* someone's hands."

"Whose hands?" Kelly pressed.

He squirmed in his chair. "I told you, ma'am. I can't recall."

Phil let out a frustrated breath. "What happened after you retrieved your rifle from the stump?"

"I kept advancing up the rise, sir, to get to the enemy."

"Did you fire your rifle at that point?"

"Not then."

"But you had fired it earlier?"

"Yes, sir. When we first climbed out of the Bradley, targets popped up in front of us. I took aim and fired."

"Was Corporal Taylor in your line of fire at any time?"

Stanley's face blanched. "No, sir."

Kelly continued to stare at the young soldier. "Ballistics identified the weapon that fired the round that killed Corporal Taylor."

Stanley didn't flinch. "Yes, ma'am."

"The bullet was shot from your weapon."

His mouth dropped open for a long moment before he shook his head. "Does that mean you think I killed him, ma'am?"

"You tell me, Private."

"I didn't do it." Sincerity filled his eyes. He turned to Phil. "Sir, the bullet may appear to have come from my gun, but I didn't kill Taylor."

"How can you be sure?"

"Because once the weapon was back in my hands, I didn't fire it again. Fact was the cease-fire was called pretty soon after that, and everything stopped, as you know."

"Did you keep the rifle with you from then on?"

"Yes, sir. Until I turned it in back here in the company area."

Kelly glanced at Phil and then closed the folder. "Thank you, Private. That's all we need for now."

Stanley stood as Phil and Kelly left the room and returned to Lieutenant Bellow's office.

"Stanley says he gave his rifle to someone for a minute or so about the time Taylor was killed," Phil explained to the platoon leader.

Bellows shook his head, his brow wrinkled with confusion. "But why would he pass off his weapon?"

"Supposedly Ramsey stumbled. He wanted to help."

"How do the men react to Stanley?" Kelly asked.

"They think he's a little out of touch with reality, but they like him, ma'am."

"He goes the extra mile," Phil mentioned.

Bellows nodded. "Yes, sir, and then some."

"But," Kelly added. "He still could have fired the fatal round. I've talked to felons who could convince you they were aboveboard on everything. Stanley seems like a good guy, but it could all be a bluff." Kelly thought of her own dad.

"You're right, ma'am, about some folks." The lieutenant nodded. "But the men and I are with Stanley round the clock. No one has ever said that he wasn't what he seemed."

"Let's talk to his squad leader," Phil suggested. "Staff Sergeant Gates was here earlier when we first arrived."

"I'll get him, sir."

As Bellows left his office, Kelly shook her head. "As much as I want to believe Stanley didn't do it, the ballistics match confirms that his weapon fired the round."

"Unless there really was a person who took the gun from him. Even a minute or so is long enough for someone to take aim and fire."

Kelly narrowed her eyes contemplating the seriousness of Phil's last statement. "If someone else fired the gun, we'd be dealing with premeditated manslaughter, or worse than that. We might we looking for a murderer."

THIRTEEN

Phil and Kelly didn't have to wait long before Bellows returned with Staff Sergeant Gates. The lieutenant invited Phil and Kelly to be seated as the squad leader stood at the side of Bellows's desk.

Phil extended his hand toward Kelly. "Special Agent McQueen and I wanted to talk to you about the live-fire exercise, Sergeant, and what you recall concerning Private Stanley."

"Yes, sir."

"How did he seem prior to the cease-fire?"

Gates lowered his head as if thinking back to the mission. "I'm not sure if you've noticed, sir, but Private Stanley can be pretty high-strung. That day, he was even more on edge than usual, which was probably due to fatigue. He had pushed himself pretty hard out in the field."

"All the men had pushed hard, Sergeant."

Gates nodded. "Yes, sir. But Stanley isn't like most of the other guys. He takes everything to heart. Wears it on his sleeve, as the saying goes."

Phil waited for the staff sergeant to continue.

"Corporal Taylor had gotten on his case a couple times over the four days in the field. Evidently, Stanley had done a pretty slipshod job of setting up the latrine tent. Corporal

Taylor came behind him and fixed the problem. Taylor could be pretty vocal if he thought someone was in the wrong. I happened to overhear him counseling Stanley."

Gates shrugged. "Hard to believe Stanley would hold that against Taylor, but you never know when someone will snap."

"Is Stanley one to hold a grudge?" Kelly asked.

"He's new to the unit, ma'am. I'm not sure how he usually reacts. I can only tell you what I saw."

"Did you see Corporal Ramsey stumble on the live-fire range as you were approaching the rise of the final hill?"

"Before the cease-fire was called?"

Kelly nodded. "That's right."

"Seems to me he lost his footing. A lot was going on. The noise of the live rounds reverberated all around us."

"Did anyone help him up?"

Gates pursed his lips. "Stanley reached out his hand and pulled him back to his feet."

"Did Private Stanley have his weapon at that time?" Phil asked.

"I couldn't tell you, sir. He should have had the weapon on him. You talked to him. What did he say?"

"That he gave his weapon to someone."

Gates rubbed his jaw. "Well, sir, it could have happened, but I didn't see it."

Phil nodded. "All right. We'll want to talk to the other members of the squad."

The sergeant nodded. "Yes, sir. I'll have them assemble in the courtyard behind this building."

One by one, Phil and Kelly questioned the other men in private. No one had seen Stanley pass off his weapon. Nor had anyone seen him aim and fire inappropriately, although each soldier confessed that, with the strain of the exercise, their focus was on the job they had been tasked to do and not on Stanley.

Phil and Kelly left the platoon area and headed back to the company headquarters. Once they were in his office with the door closed, Phil sat on the edge of his desk. "You don't think Stanley is guilty, do you, Kelly?"

"Guilty of manslaughter?" She shook her head and shrugged. "I'm not sure, Phil. I keep wondering if he's trying to cover his tracks with that story about handing the gun to someone else."

"If what he said did happen, then the person who had the gun more than likely fired the deadly round."

Kelly nodded. "And then there's only one conclusion to be drawn."

"Someone wanted to take Private Taylor's life."

"Exactly."

Phil's gut tightened. "Which means we have to determine why someone would want Corporal Taylor dead."

Before Kelly could respond, her phone rang again. "This is Special Agent McQueen."

Chaplain Sanchez's voice sounded in her ear. "I'm trying to get in touch with Phil."

"We were tied up with an interrogation and just got back to his office."

"Put me on speaker so you can both listen."

"Will do." Kelly changed the setting on her phone. She glanced at Phil. "It's Sanchez."

"Hey, Chaplain, how's it going?"

Sanchez's voice filled the office. "I'm at the funeral home waiting for Lola Taylor to arrive. She wants the service to be held Monday and needs to make the arrangements for interment today. I told her I'd stop by so we could discuss the plans."

"Where's her mother-in-law?" Kelly asked. "Phil and I were at the farmhouse earlier today, and no one answered the door. I was worried Mildred may have taken a turn for the worse and needed medical care."

"I don't think that's the case," the chaplain answered. "I asked her if she wanted someone to sit with her mother-in-law while she was at the funeral home. She said a friend would stay with Mildred."

Kelly felt a sense of relief. "So Millie's all right?"

"Evidently."

Phil glanced down at the phone. "I wasn't able to give her the money collected from the men, Chaplain."

"That's why I called. Since she's going to be at the funeral home for a while, I wondered if you could drive out here with the love offering. Knowing she had some extra cash on hand might bring her comfort. I expect her here in the next fifteen minutes or so."

Phil glanced at Kelly, who nodded in agreement.

"If we leave now, we'll get there about the same time." Phil reached for his hat as Kelly disconnected.

She returned her cell to her purse and stood. "I'm not sure if this has bearing on the investigation, Phil, but I want to see Lola again. I'm still concerned about her mother-in-law."

"I wonder if someone was in the house taking care of Mildred when we stopped by earlier."

"Maybe. But if so, why didn't the person answer the door?"

The first sergeant stood when Phil and Kelly left his office. "Sir, battalion headquarters sent over the roster of post personnel who attended the live-fire demonstration." He held out a folder. "I included it with the names of the VIPs the protocol office invited. Here's the entire list."

"Perfect timing." Phil took the file from the sergeant and

then handed it to Kelly. "You look over the complete list while I drive."

Once they were on their way, Kelly read through the names. "I've seen the list of dignitaries the protocol office invited but not the battalion add-ons."

"I doubt you'll find Kyle Foglio's name."

"You're right. I don't see him."

"The area for the dignitaries was a distance from the bleachers where the local guests were seated, Kelly. Are you sure you saw the Foglio kid? Could it have been someone who looked like him?"

"I'm sure it was Kyle. He was with a girl. She had long brown hair and was wearing a denim jacket."

"Sounds like a description that would match most teenage girls in the area."

Kelly continued to read over the names. "There's a Mrs. Meyers on the list. Is that the first sergeant's wife?"

"Probably. The battalion notified us of some cancellations and asked if we wanted to fill the slots with family members."

"Evidently she brought a guest."

"Maybe one of the other wives. The final list was compiled while we were in the field."

"There's a Valerie Davis listed with a guest. Does that name sound familiar?"

"We don't have anyone named Davis in the company, but that doesn't mean she couldn't be associated with the battalion."

Kelly punched Jamison's number into her cell. When he answered, she said, "Do me a favor and see if you can find a woman or teen named Valerie Davis. She and a guest were at the live fire."

"Kyle Foglio's girlfriend perhaps?" Jamison asked, jumping to the same conclusion as Kelly.

"That's what I'm hoping."

"I'll get back to you."

"Thanks, Jamison."

"By the way, the chief is ready for this investigation to be wrapped up so he can send your report to the commanding general."

"I need a little more time."

"I'll tell him you're tying up loose ends."

"I owe you."

"And I'll collect the next time I'm lead investigator. But, Kel, seems to me if you know the weapon, you should know who shot the round."

"The soldier says he handed his rifle to someone right before Taylor was hit."

Jamison guffawed. "Now that's convenient. And you believe him?"

"I'm not sure what I believe at this point. The soldier seems squeaky clean."

"Or perhaps a good actor?"

She shrugged. "Phil vouches for him."

"Yeah? Well, Phil doesn't want one of his men brought up on charges of manslaughter, now does he?"

Kelly bristled. No matter what Jamison believed, Phil had been forthright throughout the investigation and was as committed as she was to find out what had happened.

"I need to go, Jamison."

As Kelly disconnected, she realized the only defense Private Stanley had offered was that the rifle had been out of his sight for a minute or two. He had never questioned that the fatal round had been fired from his M-4.

As she and Jamison both knew, the soldier's story wouldn't hold up in a judicial inquiry. Private Stanley would be found guilty of fratricide whether it was intentional or not. Would Phil be found negligent, as well?

Her chest tightened, knowing she was running out of time. Kelly needed to find out what Lola Taylor was doing at the farmhouse. Somehow it tied in with Corporal Taylor's death.

FOURTEEN

The chaplain was standing outside the funeral home when Phil pulled his pickup into the parking lot and rolled down his window.

"Lola hasn't arrived yet?" he asked Sanchez.

The chaplain shook his head. "She called and said she was going to be about thirty minutes late."

Phil turned to Kelly, sitting in the passenger seat. "Shall we wait?"

Kelly glanced at her watch. "Kyle Foglio's stepmother lives nearby. Why don't we see if she's home? It shouldn't take long."

"We'll be back," Phil told the chaplain.

Following Kelly's directions, Phil found the residential area and the modest ranch at the end of the block. He pulled into the driveway and cut the engine.

Climbing out of his pickup, he glanced through the garage window. "Looks like no one is home."

Kelly pointed to the house. "Let's check out the residence while we're here. If Kyle has a key, he may have been staying here while his stepmom was gone."

Their knock went unanswered, and they saw nothing unusual when they looked through the windows.

Opening the street mailbox, Kelly peered inside. "No

mail, which means either the mailman hasn't come today or Mrs. Foglio is having it held at the post office while she's out of town."

They climbed back into the truck and retraced the route they had taken earlier. Just as they turned onto the main road, Kelly nudged Phil's arm. "Do you see what I see?"

He followed her gaze. At the far end of the next block, a late-model blue Buick had pulled to the curb. The driver handed something to a teenager who stood on the corner. He passed something back into the car, all the while glancing up and down the street and then over his shoulder.

"That's Kyle Foglio." Kelly pulled a pen and notebook from her purse. "Can you read the license plate?"

"A Georgia tag caked with mud." Phil squinted. "I can't see the number."

Kelly scooted up on the seat. "All I can make out is H8."

Phil increased his speed and approached the vehicle. The kid turned to stare in their direction. He said something to the driver of the car and then ran into a nearby alley. The car pulled away from the curb and turned right at the next intersection.

"Let me out," Kelly insisted. "You follow the car. I'll run after Kyle."

"Your leg, remember? I'll take the kid."

Pulling to the curb, Phil jumped from the truck. He raced across the street and into the alleyway. Two overturned garbage cans blocked his path.

Phil leaped over the obstacles and increased his speed. He always maxed the company PT tests and came in first in the two-mile run, but today the combat boots he wore slowed his progress. Sweat dampened his uniform.

Up ahead, the alley veered right, then left and then right again. In the maze of turns, he lost sight of Kyle.

Surely the boy was just up ahead. Another turn, this time

to the left. Rounding the corner, Phil stopped short. The alley ended at the edge of another street. Cars cruised along the thoroughfare.

Phil glanced right and then left.

A few townspeople ambled along the sidewalk, admiring the wares displayed in the shop windows. A man walked his dog. A mother pushed her baby in a stroller.

Phil blew out a series of quick breaths and then jammed his fist into his outstretched palm. The kid had disappeared.

Frustrated, Phil double-timed back to where he had left Kelly. Concern wrapped around him as he hastened toward the intersection. Kelly and his pickup were nowhere in sight.

Once Phil raced into the alleyway, Kelly slipped behind the wheel of his pickup, gunned the engine and turned right at the next intersection. The road dead-ended at a three-way stop.

On a hunch, Kelly turned left. The street led toward the river that wound along the edge of town. A cluster of small mom-and-pop shops sat tucked back from the pavement.

At the fork in the road, Kelly headed under an overpass and pulled to a stop in a gravel lot that overlooked the water. Getting out, she scanned the waterfront. A breeze picked at her hair and filled the air with the smell of the river. In the distance, she saw a small marina where a number of locals kept their boats. A handful of cars were parked in a nearby lot but not one of them was blue. Kelly had made a wrong turn and lost the person driving the car with the muddied license plate.

Kyle had been doing more than just talking. Something had been passed back and forth. Kelly had worked enough narcotics cases to know drugs had more than likely changed hands.

Not that she could prove anything, but if nothing had been

going down, then why had the kid run away? Hopefully, Phil would be able to catch up to him.

That hope vanished when Kelly approached the intersection and saw Phil standing alone. She pulled to the curb and rounded the truck to the passenger side.

Phil climbed behind the wheel. "Kyle had too much of a head start on me."

"Don't feel bad. I lost the car."

"Let's drive around and see if we can find either the kid or the Buick." They spent the next fifteen minutes cruising the town. Their eyes focused on the nooks and crannies where a teenage boy could hide. Each parking area was closely examined in hopes they'd find the blue car.

Eventually they neared the funeral home. Phil glanced at his watch. "We haven't checked the area where Mrs. Foglio lives, but I think we should stop now. The chaplain's expecting us."

"I'm beginning to wonder if we'll find the Buick parked at the funeral home."

Phil raised his brow. "You think Lola was the woman talking to Kyle?"

"They weren't talking, Phil. She was probably selling the prescription drugs that belong to her mother-in-law."

"Are you sure you're not jumping to the wrong conclusion?"

Kelly didn't like Phil's comment. "How can you say it wasn't drug-related?"

"The same way you think it was. We both saw what we wanted to see."

"I didn't make it up, Phil. Lola Taylor is acting suspicious about her mother-in-law's medical condition. My guess is she's selling Mildred's drugs on the street. Today, Kyle Foglio was buying."

Phil didn't respond, and they rode in silence to the funeral home. Kelly walked ahead of him into a small office where she stopped short. Sitting in a chair, looking cool as could be, was Lola Taylor.

Sanchez sat next to her. He glanced up and smiled. "We've been waiting for you."

Kelly turned to gaze over her shoulder as Phil entered the room and acknowledged both Lola and the chaplain.

An associate from the funeral home hustled to carry two more chairs into the room. "Ma'am, please sit down."

He unfolded the second chair. "Sir, please."

Phil helped Kelly into the chair before he sat. "Mrs. Taylor, the unit collected a love offering for you."

Before Phil could reach into his pocket, Kelly put her hand on his. "Mrs. Taylor, did you drive here?"

"No, actually I got a ride with a friend."

"A friend? Who would that be?"

"A friend from town. She dropped me off and is doing some shopping now. I'll call her when I'm ready to go home."

Phil patted Kelly's arm and lowered his voice so only she could hear. "You need to accept Mrs. Taylor's explanation."

"But—"

Kelly wasn't ready to accept any explanation that didn't add up. Lola Taylor had small-town crook written all over her, and Kelly needed to find out where she had stashed the Buick and any other pills she might be selling on the street.

Tension in the room escalated as Kelly wrapped her arms around her chest and stared at Lola. Phil gave the widow the love offering and explained how the men had wanted to help her. She seemed visibly touched and graciously accepted the money.

"Please…" Her voice was tight with emotion. "Please tell the soldiers how much I appreciate their thoughtfulness."

Fearing Kelly might say something she would later regret,

Phil mentioned he was needed back at post. Then, grabbing Kelly's hand, he ushered her outside.

"She's lying," Kelly said. "I don't believe a friend dropped her off. I'm sure she hid her car so we can't search it for her mother-in-law's prescription drugs."

He raked his hand over his short hair. "She's taking care of Mildred in her home. Didn't you say that's what you had wanted to do?"

Kelly put her hands on her hips. "And you reminded me that I couldn't have cared for my mother when I was in the military."

He nodded, realizing she was right. "You did everything you could, Kelly. I'm not saying you didn't, but it's as if you're in competition with Lola. She's living her life. You have to live yours."

"Just so she doesn't hurt Mildred."

"I doubt she would, don't you? I mean really, Kelly."

She didn't say anything until he had pulled out of the parking lot. "Let's drive around some more, Phil. I want to keep looking for the Buick."

"That you think Lola was driving?"

"No matter who was at the wheel, I need to find that car."

He turned onto one of the side streets. "Okay, you direct me."

They drove up and down a number of roads they hadn't checked earlier but without success. Finally, they turned onto the street where Mrs. Foglio lived.

"Well, I'll be." Kelly pointed to the house at the end of the block. The late-model Buick with muddied license plate was parked outside the garage. Kyle's stepmother stood at the mailbox at the edge of the road and pulled out a stack of mail.

"Looks like Mrs. Foglio finally returned home, and the mailman just made a delivery."

Phil parked in the driveway.

"Mrs. Foglio?" Kelly called to her as they stepped from the truck.

The woman turned and raised her brows. Then she nodded. "You were with the CID department on post."

"Yes, ma'am." Kelly introduced Phil. "Mrs. Foglio, we've been searching for your stepson. Did you know Kyle was back in Freemont?"

"I saw him when I drove in." She glanced at Phil's pickup. "I believe Kyle saw your truck before he ran off."

"Why did you race away from us, ma'am?"

"Kyle said you were after him." She straightened her shoulders and narrowed her eyes at Kelly. "If you must know, I didn't want to get involved. Looks like I am now. What's this about?"

"I have reason to believe Kyle entered my garage and tampered with my property."

Mrs. Foglio's gaze darkened. "Are you sure it was Kyle?"

"Agent McQueen saw your stepson a few nights ago on a back road," Phil explained. "He ran off into the woods. Someone entered her garage that night and the next, as well."

"Did you see Kyle in your garage?" the stepmother demanded.

Kelly shook her head. "No, ma'am."

"Then how do you know it was Kyle?"

Unable to answer the question, Kelly asked, "Do you know where your stepson could be staying?"

"I talked to him for about thirty seconds before you two scared him off. He didn't have time to tell me where he was sleeping, and I only had time to give him some money so he could buy something to eat."

"What did he give you, ma'am?"

"If you must know, his dirty clothes. He's been camping

out for a number of days without a chance to wash his clothing. Kyle may have problems, but he's a decent kid."

"Does Kyle have a girlfriend in the area?" Kelly pressed.

"There's a girl on post. Her name's Maddie. I can't remember her last name. She lives in the housing area near the bachelor officer quarters." Mrs. Foglio turned on her heel. "Now, if you'll excuse me, I need to unpack."

Phil and Kelly walked back to his truck. He held the door for her, then rounded the car and took a seat behind the wheel.

As he drove out of the residential area, Kelly picked up her cell and called Jamison. "I've got more information I need you to check. Kyle Foglio's stepmother said he likes a girl who lives in the noncommissioned officers' housing area behind the BOQ. See if Corporal Otis can find a teen named Maddie in that area. Another option is to check the high school."

"His stepmother was right," Phil said once she hung up. "You can't prove Kyle was in your garage."

"Now you're sounding like a lawyer." She focused on the road.

"Plus, Kelly, you've got to admit that you jumped to the wrong conclusion about Mrs. Taylor. She wasn't selling Mildred's drugs."

Kelly crossed her arms over her chest. "Maybe we should head back to post so I can finish up the investigation on your live-fire mission. The way it looks right now, I'd have to say the accident was a direct result of fatigue on the part of your soldiers."

She was lashing out at him for no reason except she was frustrated and on edge. He had pushed Kelly too far, and she was reacting. She was a good CID agent, but she'd just been shoved into a corner, where evidently she didn't want to be.

Regrettably, she believed Phil had made a very serious

mistake. He thought back to when he was a kid. His dad had made a mistake that had cost two men their lives.

"The apple never falls far from the tree." Once again, he heard the words Freemont police officer Tim Simpson had spoken. Only this time, he realized they just might be true.

FIFTEEN

Kelly admired her boss. Chief Agent in Charge Craig Wilson was competent and dedicated. He knew the ins and outs of law enforcement and felony crime, which was the CID's main focus, but he also knew people and how to get the job done.

At the present moment, his full lips were pursed and his dark eyes stared at her over the top of his reading glasses. For some reason, she felt like a schoolkid standing in front of the principal.

"Sir, I'd like more time on this case."

"Ballistics identified the weapon, and you've talked to the soldier involved."

"Yes, sir, but as I mentioned, there seems to be some question as to whether he fired the fatal round. I told you Stanley claims he handed the gun to another soldier."

"Who at this point remains unidentified?"

Chief Wilson was right, of course. "That's correct, sir. I haven't been able to find the person to whom Private Stanley supposedly handed his rifle."

"The key word is *supposedly*. If the soldier wanted to deflect suspicion away from himself, introducing a nonidentifiable 'other' person is a logical tactic."

"I understand that, sir. The company commander, Captain

Thibodeaux, says the private works hard and is trustworthy. Chaplain Sanchez has talked with him. The young man has a deep faith, and the chaplain vouched for him, as well."

"Which doesn't mean he didn't make a mistake at live fire."

"That's correct, sir."

"Is there anything else that plays into your investigation?"

"Just a gut feeling, sir."

Wilson raised his brow and waited for Kelly to explain. She wanted to give her boss enough information to understand her feelings about the case, but she didn't want to dig a hole she couldn't get out of later if her gut was wrong.

No matter how strongly she believed something was going on with Lola Taylor, Kelly needed hard evidence for her report that Wilson would send up the chain of command to the commanding general. Since the governor seemed to be interested in this case, the determination she came to could go all the way to the state level, as well.

"Taylor lived on his mother's property north of town, sir. The neighboring property contained a series of traps large enough to snare a human being. I'm trying to determine who owns that land."

"But how does that play into Taylor's death?"

"At this point, I'm not sure. But his mother was released from the local nursing home last year. Taylor's wife cared for her while he was deployed and now the older woman is bedridden and unable to communicate."

"A lot can happen to a person in a year, Agent McQueen."

"Yes, sir, but—"

What she really wanted to say was that Lola Taylor was hiding something and was less than forthright about her mother-in-law's medical care. She took her to a doctor suspected of criminal activity and seemed to push sleeping pills to quiet the older woman. All of which went along with

Kelly's gut feeling, and in no way was anything she would mention to Wilson at this point.

"Sir, if you could give me a little more time. A number of items are still up in the air, which I'd like to follow to their logical conclusion, before I complete my report."

He sniffed and then nodded. "I don't know if you've seen the Atlanta papers, but the media is having a heyday with Corporal Taylor's death. They're claiming a military cover-up."

"I, ah, haven't seen the papers, sir." No hiding the fact that she was getting deeper into a sticky situation that became more complicated the longer the case remained unresolved.

"Well, I hope you tune into what's happening at the state capitol. The governor wants a speedy resolution to this case, as does the post commanding general. Tomorrow is the post Hail and Farewell social gathering at the club. The general will, no doubt, corner me and ask when the investigation will be completed. I'd like to tell him it will be wrapped up by the following day, Saturday. That gives you forty-eight hours to tie up those loose ends."

"Yes, sir." Forty-eight hours wasn't long. Hopefully it would be long enough.

"Sir, if Private Stanley did discharge the bullet that killed Corporal Taylor, it was accidental." Phil stood in front of his battalion commander's desk, trying to make a case for Stanley's innocence.

"You're basing that on his allegation about another person taking control of his weapon just before Taylor was shot?"

"Well, sir, the so-called other person hasn't materialized, but Stanley's sure he passed his weapon back to someone."

"Yet no one in the squad can confirm his statement."

"That's correct, sir." Phil felt he was losing the battle with Lieutenant Colonel Knowlton. "Chaplain Sanchez is with him, sir. He's had counseling training, and he's trying to see if something else can come to light."

"Knowing Chaplain Sanchez, he's probably praying with the kid."

If not for the seriousness of the situation, Phil would have smiled. His commander was right. The chaplain had mentioned praying with the private.

In Phil's opinion, prayer wouldn't improve Stanley's memory, but the chaplain's concern for the soldier could do a world of good. Plus, if the private had fabricated the story to cover his own guilt, getting right with the Lord might make him realize he needed to admit the truth.

"What's the CID agent's take on the situation?" the lieutenant colonel asked.

At this point, Phil wasn't sure what Kelly believed. "She's still actively investigating the case and plans to have a decision soon, sir."

Knowlton nodded. "What's she like?"

"Ah—" Phil hesitated, not knowing how forthright he should be with his commander.

Truth was she was a career warrant officer committed to serving her country. Certainly not the type of woman Phil should be interested in, yet Kelly had occupied his attention ever since she had sallied into his life at the live-fire range.

Beware, logic kept warning him, filling his mind with memories of a young boy whose mother left him for a better job. Strong though he wanted to be, his heart got the upper hand and overrode all his good intentions to remain unaffected by the CID agent.

Phil cleared his throat and attempted to come up with an opinion that would not reveal his true feelings. "Sir, she's as determined as I am to get to the bottom of what happened. To Agent McQueen, the job comes first."

"Sounds like high praise, Phil. I'm glad to hear it. I've

heard talk from some of the single officers. They've said the same thing about being committed to her job 24/7. That's exactly who we want leading this investigation."

"Yes, sir."

"I've also heard she's an excellent marksman."

Phil nodded. "I believe she outshot the other contenders in the post-wide sharp shooting contest last year."

"Now that's impressive. Let's hope she's also speedy with her determination. The commanding general called the brigade commander and put a little pressure on him to ensure everything is wrapped up as soon as possible."

"That's my desire, as well."

Knowlton nodded. "Good, that means we're on the same page." He glanced at the calendar on his desk. "The Hail and Farewell is tomorrow night, Friday. The commanding general will open his remarks around sixteen hundred hours. You'll be there?"

"Four o'clock. Of course, sir."

"Let me know when Agent McQueen comes to a decision."

"Yes, sir."

With a brisk salute, Phil left the commander's office and headed back to his own headquarters. He needed to tell Kelly that pressure might be coming to bear in the next day or so.

She had mentioned a scheduled meeting with Chief Agent in Charge Wilson. When Phil called the CID office, Jamison answered. "What's up, Captain?"

"Is Kelly around? She said she had a meeting with your boss."

"She left his office a short while ago, but I'm not sure where she is now. She looked like she had a lot on her mind."

"Then I have a hunch where she might be."

Jamison laughed. "If you're thinking what I'm thinking, you're right. Where does Kelly always go when she's stressed?"

Phil pulled into the parking lot of the indoor shooting range and spied Kelly's Corolla near the door.

Stepping inside, he caught sight of her on the far firing lane. She held her Sig Sauer in both hands and was aiming at a target downrange. As he neared, he realized she was hitting the center mark with every shot.

She couldn't hear him approach with the ear protection she wore, so he stood to the side and watched as she fired one round after another.

Phil had to admire her ability, but he also wondered why she was so obsessive about her shooting. Once she lowered her weapon and took off her protective ear coverings, he approached her.

As Kelly turned, recognition spread over her face. "How long have you been standing here?"

"Long enough to be impressed with your ability."

She shrugged off his compliment. "Target practice goes along with being a CID agent."

He glanced at the other lanes. "I don't see Jamison here."

"Maybe he was born a good marksman." She holstered her weapon and wiped the palms of her hands on her slacks. "I've got to work to keep my skill sharp."

"You're more than sharp, Kelly." He glanced at the target. "You're dead-on with every shot."

She wrinkled her brow. "I'm not sure I like your choice of words."

"Dead-on?"

"I practice so I can deter crime, Phil. The last thing I want is to fatally wound someone, even a perpetrator. Not that I wouldn't if I had to in order to save an innocent person's life."

"I thought cops always shoot to kill."

"Not this one."

"If you're not tied up tonight, I could bring over another pizza."

She shook her head. "Thanks, but I've got work to do."

"On the investigation?"

Kelly nodded. "Wilson wants everything wrapped up within forty-eight hours. I need to input information into the file and start on the final report."

"But you need to eat, and I promise not to distract you."

"I'm sorry, Phil, but the job comes first."

The words burned in his memory. His mother had often said the same thing. Then one day she'd walked out of his life. He'd come home from school and found a note saying she had received a transfer and that she would contact him later. He'd never heard from her again.

He had thought Kelly was different from his mother. Now he wasn't so sure.

A strange feeling wrapped around Kelly as she drove away from the firing range. She glanced in her rearview mirror and saw Phil still sitting in his pickup.

He had said a hasty goodbye after she'd made the comment about needing to get work done this evening. Without as much as a backward glance, he'd climbed into his truck.

In a way, she felt hurt. Yet a part of her knew she had probably been too abrupt, as well. Seems they both had issues.

Her phone rang as she was still trying to determine why she was upset about Phil. "This is Special Agent McQueen."

Officer Simpson's voice came over the phone. "Sorry it's taken me a while to track down information about that land you were interested in."

"Not a problem." Actually, she had decided to go into

town and do a search of the county land records if she hadn't heard back from him by morning.

"The guy who holed up in that deserted trailer called himself Catfish Ryan."

She smiled. "He liked to fish?"

"That's right. Even more, he liked to have fish fries out at his campsite. Evidently folks would come from all around."

"For the fish?"

"For the betting. He ran cockfights on his property for a number of years."

A sense of euphoria swept over Kelly. Maybe she was on the right track, after all.

"Never built himself a home. Told some of the people I talked to that he wanted to be able to get up and go at a minute's notice. Seems he did just that for a number of years before he returned to Freemont."

"So he was the old codger who lived in the deserted trailer?"

"Probably so. From what I hear, Catfish stayed clear of the law and was a regular recluse. Doubt many folks knew anyone lived out there."

"What happened to him?"

"The people I talked to haven't seen him recently. He may have headed north again."

"What about the Taylors? Did they like their neighbor?"

"That's the funny thing. I wouldn't have found out except one of the gals who knew Catfish let it slip that he has a sister. She's been under the weather and doesn't get out much anymore."

"Go on," Kelly encouraged.

"The sister's name is Millie. Millie Ryan."

Kelly shoved the phone closer to her ear as Simpson continued. "Millie married a man named Taylor. They had one son."

"Rick Taylor," Kelly filled in. "Who died in a live-fire accident two days ago."

"Strange coincidence, eh?" Simpson said.

She nodded. "Do you believe in coincidence, Officer Simpson?"

"Nope."

"What about gut feelings?"

"What cop doesn't?"

"Amen to that," Kelly said before she disconnected.

She didn't have time to go home and work on her report. Everything was falling into place. All she needed was to tie up some of the loose ends.

SIXTEEN

If Kelly didn't want pizza for dinner, maybe Chinese would work. At least that's what Phil hoped as he picked up the carry-out order and drove to her house.

Call him stubborn, but he wanted to see Kelly and wouldn't take no for an answer. But when he pulled into her driveway, he realized she may not have wanted him around for a very good reason.

The house sat dark and empty. Stepping from his truck, he walked to the window and peered inside the empty garage. Kelly hadn't mentioned going anyplace or that she had a date, although the latter left a sour taste in his mouth.

Getting back in his truck, Phil pulled out of the drive and headed to State Road 15, which he followed for about a mile before he eased his truck off the pavement and onto the path that wound deep into the woods.

From the road no one would realize the narrow dirt road skirted the vacant property and continued on to the Taylor farm. How much farther it went, Phil wasn't sure. However, he was sure that Kelly suspected Lola of not giving her mother-in-law adequate care. Plus, she believed the Foglio teen might be using the deserted trailer as a place to bed down.

If the kid had attempted to break in to Kelly's property

again, she might have gone after him. Alone in the dark, and that worried Phil. Especially after the shots that had been fired the last time they'd been in the area.

Although Kelly was a CID agent and the best marksman on post, she could still be outnumbered and overpowered, and that made him uneasy.

She could also be out with one of the young, single officers on post. Or a civilian from Freemont. Maybe a guy who wanted to settle down and start a family.

Phil groaned at that thought. Was Kelly interested in having children? Not that he'd bring that up in conversation no matter how well he got to know her.

The deserted trailer appeared to his right. The moon cast the area in light. He braked to a stop and watched for anything that would indicate the property was occupied.

On the far edge of the clearing, a large buck stepped from the darkness, his antlers visible in the moonlight. Behind him a doe and fawn grazed. Had he and Kelly jumped to a very wrong decision about the snares, when in reality they had been set to capture game?

Perhaps their imaginations had gone wild with the investigation, as well. If Stanley's rifle had fired accidentally, the investigation could be wrapped up in a day or two. Phil would have his hand slapped and perhaps something written in his Officer's Efficiency Report about what had happened under his command.

The black mark on his record would mean he wouldn't be selected for promotion. Enough officers with outstanding records were vying for major. No reason for the promotion board to choose a captain with a stain on his past.

Maybe he should have canceled the four days in the field for his unit when he received the live-fire tasking. Or at least cut the field time down by half. That way his men would have been more alert for the mission and better able to make a good showing for the visiting dignitaries.

But they would have missed two days of training. Money was tight in the army. The training schedule had been approved. Phil wouldn't let time in the field slip through his fingertips just to make the governor happy.

No matter what Kelly determined about the incident and no matter what his commander and the commanding general decided, Phil had done the right thing. Even if it cost him his career in the army.

As hard as it was to think of leaving Fort Rickman and returning to civilian life, another thought tangled through his mind. Even harder than leaving the military would be to leave Kelly. Somehow over the past few days, she had taken hold of his thoughts. If he were completely honest, he might realize she'd taken hold of his heart, as well.

Kelly peered at the farmhouse, searching for any sign of activity. Mildred's room had been dark for the past hour, but the lights in the main area of the house spilled into the backyard and over the caged roosters that, so far, the neighbor had not picked up.

If Kelly was lucky, he might show up tonight. That is, if there was a neighbor.

Her hands were stiff from the cold, and her injured leg ached from the dropping temperature. She needed to return to her car and hunker down there.

Stepping quietly through the leaves, she retraced her steps and pulled open the door. A strange smell wafted past her. She sniffed, slipped into the driver's seat and screamed.

Luckily not a loud scream, more like a startled yip.

Phil sat in the passenger's seat with a Cheshire cat grin on his face visible in the moonlight. "Sorry, I scared you, but I wanted to prove my point."

Kelly had automatically reached for her holstered weapon. Now she eased her hand away from her gun and patted her chest, hoping to calm her heart, which was on a frantic path to cardiac arrest.

"Prove your point about what?" she asked once she found her voice.

"You left yourself open for trouble by keeping the car door ajar."

She waved her hand in the air to discredit his concern. "Noise travels in the quiet. I didn't want Lola to hear it slam closed."

"And what about Kyle Foglio?"

"The trailer was empty. I checked."

Phil shook his head with frustration. "The kid was roaming through these woods the first night you saw him, Kelly. He could be anywhere. And what about those shots? Have you already forgotten the three rounds and my broken taillight?"

"Okay, okay." She sank down into the seat. "I messed up. But I was more worried about Mildred than I was about Kyle, or a hunter who left the area as soon as he heard the police sirens. Plus, I wanted to see what Lola was up to."

Kelly glanced over her shoulder and searched the darkness. "Where's your truck?"

"In a cluster of pines where it can't be spotted. You, on the other hand, didn't cover your tracks, as well. I came out here thinking you went after Kyle Foglio. But the clearing was deserted. Then I spotted your Corolla with the door open."

"Which you already mentioned."

"It bears repeating, Kelly. Anyone who happened by could have crawled inside this car and been lying in wait when you slid behind the wheel. Luckily, tonight it happened to be me instead of someone who wanted to do you harm."

She sighed, knowing Phil was right. "I wasn't using my head."

"Exactly my point. But I'll cut you a little slack. After all, you were probably hungry."

"What?"

He reached into the backseat and pulled up a brown paper bag. "I brought Chinese."

"Which I thought I smelled." She jabbed his arm. "I told you not to buy me dinner."

"At the time, we were talking about pizza. I decided lo mein and sweet-and-sour pork might be a nice change of pace."

"Actually, I am hungry." Kelly smiled as he handed her a container. The sweet mix of ginger and brown sugar made her mouth water.

They ate in relative silence, both of them enjoying the rich Asian cuisine. Once their empty containers had been shoved back in the bag, Kelly realized the temperature had dropped even more. She pulled her navy jacket around her waist.

"If you're getting cold, I could turn on the heater." She reached for the key in the ignition.

Phil grabbed her hand and pointed to the farmhouse.

Kelly followed his gaze and saw Lola standing on her back steps. Arms wrapped around her chest, she stared into the wooded area where the Toyota Corolla was parked.

"Do you think she sees us?" Kelly leaned closer to Phil.

"I don't know how she could. From her angle, we're hidden by the undergrowth."

"Looks like she's searching for something or someone."

"With the temperature dropping, she's not out there just for fresh air."

Kelly shivered, and Phil's arms wrapped around her. "You've been in the cold too long." He pulled her closer. "And that jacket isn't heavy enough."

"I'm fine," she insisted.

Lola stepped back inside, but Kelly didn't move. She was enjoying the warmth of Phil's arms and the sense of security they provided.

"Are you still convinced Lola is involved with something suspect?" His breath fanned Kelly's cheek as he spoke.

"She isn't acting like a grieving widow. In fact, she reminds me of a conniving gold digger or a small-time crook, with her raised eyebrows and attempts to keep her mother-in-law holed up in the back bedroom."

Kelly told him about Catfish Ryan and his relationship to Mildred Taylor. "It's a tie-in, Phil, which is what I've been looking for."

"Are you sure you're not transposing your grief for your mom onto Mildred?"

"Maybe," Kelly admitted. "But if the geriatric clinic and Millie's physician are being investigated by the Labor Department for Medicare fraud, the doctor might not be attentive to Mildred's real medical needs. Oxycodone sells on the street for a good price."

"And that plays into Corporal Taylor's death?"

"Crime fosters crime. Make a bad decision concerning a little thing and it becomes easier to fudge on something bigger. If Catfish was involved in cockfights and Lola has four roosters in her backyard, we've got a connection."

He rubbed his hand over her arm and let out a deep breath as he stared into the night. Finally, he said, "My father took money from the company he worked for to buy big-ticket items he never could have afforded otherwise. For a long time, I blamed myself."

"You thought you were the reason he embezzled from his company?"

Phil nodded. "I thought I had asked for too much as a kid. Actually, my dad planted ideas in my mind for the things he planned to buy. When he came home with a television or new sound system—one time it was a sports car—I thought I had been the one who first asked for the items."

"What about your mom?"

Phil's fingers caressed Kelly's cheek. "My aunt mentioned money had been tight and credit cards had been overcharged repeatedly. All issues that must have bothered my business-minded mother. Maybe she tired of my father's life-of-the-party ideas."

Gazing down at Kelly, Phil added, "He was big on letting the good times roll, the typical Cajun you talk about your father being, only, my dad lived that to the max."

"How did he get caught?"

"By taking money that was earmarked for some new safety equipment. His company did office cleaning, which included external window washing. New scaffolding was needed, but my father said the old equipment had been upgraded. He got away with it until a crew was out on a particularly windy day." Phil shook his head. "They were fifteen stories up. The scaffold broke and two men died in the fall."

"Oh, Phil, I'm so sorry."

"Everything came out. My dad had siphoned off funds from the company for years. Looking back, they found a number of safety issues that hadn't been fixed, yet he had signed off on them. On paper the company looked compliant with all the new safety regulations, which wasn't the case."

"And your dad went to prison?"

Phil nodded. "My mother left him right after the accident. At that point, he was still claiming that every precaution had been in place."

"She probably suspected the truth."

"Or was just fed up with his lies. She transferred jobs to another state."

"And left you with her sister?"

"My father's sister."

Kelly looked up into his eyes and saw the pain of his past and the guilt he had carried for his father's actions.

"I always wanted a father who loved me," she whispered. "A man I could look up to and admire. A guy who tried to do the right thing, even when times got tough."

He nodded in agreement. "Yeah, me, too."

"You're that kind of guy, Phil."

His eyes opened a bit wider, and she felt him stir. Then his lips quirked into a smile. "You think of me as a father?"

She laughed until the levity left his face, replaced with something so intense it took her breath. The defenses she had put in place long ago dropped, and all the warmth and love she wanted to be able to give to someone special welled up within her until she was overcome with a need to draw closer to Phil.

She wrapped her arm around his neck.

Her heart pounded in sync with his as he lowered his lips. The gentleness of his touch absorbed the last of her caution. All she could think of was how perfect it felt to be wrapped in Phil's arms and to give herself totally to him.

Phil pulled Kelly closer, losing himself in the exquisite warmth of her embrace. Despite the warning that tried to surface, he took her lips again, feeling a sense of completeness as she molded into his arms.

He kissed her cheek, her neck and the edge of her ear and wove his fingers through her hair, which smelled like flowers and sunshine.

Phil opened his eyes to take in her beauty and saw movement on the floor below. His stomach lurched and his muscles went rigid.

Kelly pulled back ever so slightly. "What's wrong?"

"Don't move," he whispered through tight lips.

She started to shift, but his hold on her tightened. "I said don't move."

"Phil—" Turning her head slightly to follow his gaze, she gasped.

Something slithered out from under the driver's seat. Even in the darkness, he recognized the red and yellow bands of the Eastern coral snake.

Kelly's feet were dangerously close to the snake's head, which would strike if provoked. With his right hand, Phil reached for the passenger door handle and eased it open.

"Don't make any sudden movements. I'll lift you as you edge your feet away from the floorboard."

Kelly nodded almost imperceptibly.

She was tense in his arms. One wrong move and the snake would strike. Slowly, she pulled up her feet.

"Good job," he whispered. Phil lifted her up and over him until she was on the ground outside the car.

The snake curled the tip of its tail, a technique to confuse its prey.

Kelly tugged on Phil's sleeve. "It's ready to attack."

Phil lunged out the door. He expected to feel the painful bite, but the snake struck the leather seat instead.

Kelly gasped.

Phil pushed her away from the door. "Stand back." As they watched, the snake slithered out the door and disappeared under a pile of fallen leaves.

"How did it get into my car?"

"Your door was ajar," Phil reminded her. "Although I don't think the snake crawled in on its own. Someone put it there, Kelly. Probably while you were watching the farmhouse."

Her eyes opened a bit wider. Then she glanced into the darkness. "Kyle Foglio?"

"Or someone else who wants you out of the way."

She turned toward the Taylor home. In the excitement

over the snake, they had both failed to notice Lola standing on her back porch.

"I have a feeling she knows we're out here," Phil said. "She may know about the snake as well, if she talked Kyle Foglio into putting it in your car."

"But why?"

Phil watched Kelly's expression change as she realized the answer to her own question. "Lola Taylor wants me dead."

SEVENTEEN

"I don't think you should stay here alone," Phil said once they were back at Kelly's house.

She shook her head. "I'm not going to be scared off my own property."

"Then call the police, Kelly."

She raised her hands. "And what would I tell them? That I was snooping around where I shouldn't have been, and a snake slithered into my car? I don't have evidence that Lola Taylor or Kyle Foglio had anything to do with the snake."

"Yet you thought they were both involved when you saw Lola on her back steps."

Kelly nodded. "It's hard to believe she didn't know we were out there."

"And if she's somehow tied in with Kyle Foglio—"

"Okay." Kelly shrugged. "She could be paying him to do her dirty work."

"Which makes sense. She wants to scare you off so she has Kyle leave the cut piece of rope and the possum."

"But the garage door opened that first night before she would have ever suspected I could cause problems."

"The kid saw you follow him. He wanted to scare you. Once Lola found out you were snooping around, she might have encouraged Kyle to push you a little harder. He may have been the one firing the rifle, as well."

Kelly raked her hand through her hair and shook her head. "We don't have evidence to substantiate any of this, Phil. It's pure conjecture, which wouldn't hold up with the local cops, or in a court of law."

"So we need to keep an eye on Lola to see if she tips her hand. Monday's the funeral. Surely, she won't be going anyplace until after that's over."

"The post Hail and Farewell is tomorrow night. Wilson wants to tell the general that I'll have my investigation completed on Saturday."

"Have you come to a conclusion yet about the incident?"

"Not yet."

"What about Stanley?"

She didn't want to be pushed, especially after what had happened in the car. She was still reeling from Phil's kisses. Kelly needed space to clear her mind and allow her emotions to get back on an even keel.

"I don't think we should even be talking about the decision at this point, Phil."

He raised his brow. "Meaning what?"

"Meaning I don't want you to influence my decision."

He bristled. "Is that what you think I was doing in the car?"

"You mean when you were kissing me?"

He nodded.

"I..." She couldn't let him know how much she had wanted him to kiss her. Now she realized her mistake. Phil was the type of guy who played with women's hearts. He turned on the Cajun charm when he needed something, and right now, Phil needed a good decision on the investigation. He had almost said as much.

No wonder he had come on to Kelly in the car. His actions

had nothing to do with the way he felt. He'd seen her need and played into it, kissing her repeatedly until she couldn't think straight and was ready to give him her heart.

Just as her mother had done with her dad. Just as Kelly had tried to do each time her father had come back into her life as a child.

Her father hadn't wanted her love. That had become blatantly clear the night he had broken into their house high on drugs. She had blocked out so much about what had happened, but she could never forget the vicious names he'd called her mother, and her as well, which proved he was a crazed lunatic who had to be stopped.

No, Kelly wouldn't let her attraction to Captain Jean Philippe Thibodeaux cause her to make another mistake.

"Go home, Phil. You've done enough tonight."

"What?"

"I don't need you to protect me. I can take care of myself."

"I know you can, but—"

"No buts. It's late and we both have a full day of work tomorrow."

Pain sliced across his face, and she realized her words had been too caustic, but she couldn't take them back. If she did, she might throw herself into his arms again and never stop kissing him.

People often said she was her mother's daughter because of the similarity of their looks, but the resemblance ended on the surface. Kelly had learned long ago to steel her heart, which is exactly what she had to do with Phil. Better to close him out of her life now than to let him break her heart later.

Without another word, he turned on his heels and stormed out of her house. The door slammed behind him. She pulled back the edge of the living room curtain, seeing the one working taillight disappear into the distance, leaving her totally alone with only the memory of his kisses, a memory she'd never be able to forget no matter how much she tried to cut him out of her life.

Phil pressed down on the accelerator and went from zero to sixty in the amount of time it took to bite the inside of his cheek to keep from screaming.

He should have known Kelly wasn't any different than his mother. Both women were focused on their jobs. The military came first. Hadn't Kelly implied that very thing the other night? Only he'd been too smitten to realize what it meant for him.

Tonight, there had been no skirting the issue. She didn't want anything to do with him. Yet she'd seemed interested when they'd been together in her car. Truth be told, he had been more than interested.

The moment their lips had met, he'd felt a sense of completeness sweep over him, as if all the pain in his past had been wiped away. Something inside him had soared, and for the first time, he felt free to be the man he wanted to be. The fear of failure that always hovered over him had disappeared with Kelly in his arms. He felt ten feet tall and strong enough to slay a fire-eating dragon if need be, to prove his love for Kelly.

Then the snake had changed that emotionally charged moment. Ironic that a snake had tempted Adam and Eve in the Garden. They had followed the deceiver and disobeyed the Lord, which meant they had to leave the Garden.

Phil had cut the Lord out of his life long ago. Instead of turning to God for answers, Phil had believed the Almighty had allowed his father to fail. Living with Aunt Eleanor had softened his heart, but he had never been able to accept the Lord's forgiveness and redemption.

Now his eyes were open to the truth, and he saw his dad

as a flawed sinner who had made terrible mistakes. Phil was young at the time. He wasn't to blame for his dad's actions no matter how many things he had begged for as a kid. His father was the adult and should have made good decisions on his son's behalf.

And Phil's mother? Maybe she got tired of her husband never being satisfied with what he had. Eleanor said his mom had left with a mountain of debt piled high on her shoulders from his dad's overspending ways. She had probably known she couldn't care for her child financially. Yes, she had made a mistake leaving Phil, but now he saw her as a woman who needed help instead of a woman he had tried to hate for so long.

"Forgive her, Father," he prayed.

Kelly's face floated through his mind, and he saw with clarity the barriers she had placed around her heart. She had been hurt so much by her Cajun dad that she was overly cautious when it came to men. He shook his head and lowered his speed, feeling his frustration start to ebb along with a new realization of why she had lashed out at him tonight.

If actions meant anything, she did have feelings for him. The way she had kissed him proved it. He wouldn't allow words spoken in haste, no matter how cutting, to change his feelings for her.

Tomorrow, he would try to convince Kelly that she needed to work through whatever had happened with her father.

Please, Lord, let me be able to convince her that she needs to be free of her past in order to live more fully in the moment. Only then will she be able to embrace the future.

More than anything, Phil hoped Kelly's future would include him.

Kelly was tied up most of the next day with meetings at CID headquarters that had nothing to do with the live-fire investigation. In a spare moment, she called Officer Simpson to see if he or the other officers had found anyone near the trailer the day before.

"Not a soul, but hunters wander back there all the time."

Kelly didn't believe a hunter had fired the shots. "Do you have any more information about Catfish Ryan?"

"I was just fixin' to call you about that."

"Oh?"

"Talking about Catfish and that property of his got me wondering. I stopped by the county land bureau and had a little chat with a clerk I know."

"What did you find out?"

"Catfish doesn't own the land."

"So who does?"

"Turns out the clerk's aunt went to high school with Catfish. According to her, he was a shiftless kid who got into trouble. His parents weren't particularly interested in leaving their farm to him."

Kelly nodded. "So they left their land to Mildred?"

"Everyone presumed Catfish owned the land because he parked the trailer there, but the deed for the Taylor farm and the property with the clearing belongs to Mildred Taylor."

"Now isn't that interesting."

"Especially so since a big development company is looking to buy a large parcel of property near Freemont. As you probably know, Uncle Sam's assigning more military units to Fort Rickman. Housing on post will be at a premium, and home sales in town will bring top dollar. A representative from the development company picked up the plat for all the Taylor property a few weeks ago."

Kelly raised her brow. "Mildred would stand to make a sizeable amount of money if her land sold to the developers."

"That's right. Although from what you've said, she's too infirm to negotiate that significant of a business dealing."

"But someone else could make the decisions for her. Maybe a daughter-in-law who probably has a power of attorney for her mother-in-law, especially since her husband had been recently deployed. Lola would have needed to make decisions about Mildred's banking and business dealings while her husband was in Afghanistan. Seems to me, now that Corporal Taylor is dead, if something happens to Mildred the land will go to Lola."

"There's nothing illegal about that," Simpson cautioned. "Although if Catfish is still alive and there wasn't a will, he might get a share of Mildred's estate, as well."

"Has anyone seen Catfish?"

"Not that I can determine."

"Maybe you need to start looking for him."

Before Simpson hung up, he asked, "How's that garage of yours?"

"Locked up tight as a drum."

"And your house? Did you ever get those dead bolts?"

"Not yet."

As they disconnected, Kelly realized she'd left in such a hurry this morning with her mind still reeling from what had happened with Phil the night before that she hadn't engaged the lock on the kitchen door.

No reason to be concerned. The garage door had slammed shut into the locked position. At least, she thought it had.

Kelly tried to work on the investigation, but the memory of Phil's kisses kept getting in the way. She let out a deep breath and refocused on her report. Taylor's death appeared to be accidental, yet the fact that Stanley talked about a second person having possession of the gun made her wonder if the private wasn't trying to cover his own guilt.

Once she submitted her findings, the report would go up the chain of command to the commanding general, who would institute an Article 15-6 investigation to determine whether a court-martial should be convened.

More problems for Phil, as well as Private Stanley. From what the chaplain indicated, Stanley put his faith in God. Long ago, Kelly had prayed for God's protection, but He hadn't listened to her then. What made her think that He would listen to Stanley now?

And Phil? If the soldier was charged with negligence, Phil's record could be adversely affected.

Would he blame Kelly? She shook her head and sighed. Did it matter? She and Phil had disagreed last night. He was past tense. All she had to be concerned about now was her job.

If she was lucky, she wouldn't see Phil again. But somehow she didn't feel lucky. Instead, she felt very sad.

EIGHTEEN

That evening at the Hail and Farewell, Kelly scanned the crowd of military personnel looking for Phil. She ordered a soda from the bar and overheard a couple of lieutenants talking about the case.

"Supposedly Thibodeaux's hot on some chick."

"No way." The second guy took a pull on his beer.

"Someone said she's a real looker. She'll probably be with him tonight."

Kelly moved away from the men, feeling another stab of betrayal. Phil had a girlfriend? If so, Kelly had been right all along about the Cajun.

The commanding general asked everyone to focus their attention to the head of the room where he welcomed those gathered and began to introduce the new people assigned to post. Following the "hails," the general would farewell those moving on to their next duty station. Many of the parting personnel would give impromptu speeches to thank the people with whom they had served. A bronze eagle would be presented to each departing service member as a token of gratitude from the military community.

Kelly glanced at her watch. The Hail and Farewell started shortly after 4:00 p.m. and would last for a couple hours. What was keeping Phil? Usually he was always on time.

Maybe he was tied up with his girlfriend. The thought made her stomach sour.

The guy she had overheard at the bar nudged his friend and pointed to the main door on the left. "There's Thibodeaux now. Get a load of the redhead he's with."

Kelly's heart dropped, and her cheeks burned. She turned to look in the direction the man pointed.

Easy enough to spot Phil. He always stood out in the crowd. Tonight he looked even more handsome in his uniform. Tears stung Kelly's eyes as her gaze fell on the tall, slender redhead at his side. The woman flashed a smile at Phil and her hand patted his arm as he ushered her into the crowded room. A number of the officers turned to look her way and nodded their approval.

Kelly couldn't take the pain that cut through her heart. She had tried to protect herself from never being the other woman as she always suspected her mother had been, but she hadn't done a good enough job. Whatever Kelly had imagined had been between her and Phil was over, if there had been anything in the first place.

Kelly knew better than to give her heart to a Cajun, but she'd done exactly that. Now, just like her mother, she had to live with that mistake for the rest of her life.

Phil searched the crowded ballroom, hoping to see Kelly. The Post Hail and Farewell was a command performance, and he had expected she would be there.

He spied Jamison in the rear of the room. As much as he wanted to ask the CID agent about Kelly's whereabouts, the general was talking, and Phil didn't want to shove his way through the throng of military personnel that were listening to the post commander.

A couple guys he knew sidled over and smiled expectantly at the redhead Phil was escorting.

"So who's your girlfriend?" one of them whispered so only Phil could hear.

Mildly irritated by the lieutenant's brashness, Phil put his finger to his lips. "Shh. It's not polite to talk when the CG has the floor."

As Phil's gaze turned back to the commanding general, he caught sight of Kelly and tried to get her attention across the room. Either she didn't see him or was ignoring him. Hopefully, it wasn't the latter.

Skillfully navigating his way to the opposite side of the ballroom, Phil approached her and touched her arm. Kelly pursed her lips and continued to stare straight ahead.

"Something wrong?" he asked.

"The general's talking," she whispered out of the side of her mouth, just as he had cautioned the young lieutenant minutes earlier.

"Listen, I'm sorry about the way we parted last night. I acted like a jerk."

"It's okay, Phil."

"No, I need to explain."

"There's nothing to explain. Now, if you'll excuse me, I need to talk to Jamison." Kelly turned on her heel and headed deeper into the crowd.

Phil let out a lungful of air. Evidently she didn't want to talk about what had happened. He'd try again after the general finished the hails and farewells. Surely, he could convince Kelly to give him another chance, maybe over dinner.

Weaving his way back through the crowd, Phil smiled as he saw the lieutenants continuing to fawn over Sylvia Watters. He'd let them make fools of themselves before he explained she was his college roommate's fiancée. Phil would have the last laugh on them, but then he looked around the ballroom and could no longer see Kelly. The lieutenant's comment about Sylvia being his girlfriend floated through his mind. Had Kelly come to the same incorrect conclusion as the young officer? If so, no wonder she was upset.

Phil shook his head and sighed with frustration. Evidently the last laugh was on him.

Kelly's eyes stung as she drove away from the club and headed back to Freemont and her house. Passing the nursing home, she was overwhelmed once again with grief for her mother and with the pain of seeing the redhead with Phil.

Tears rolled down her cheeks, and she had to blink to see her driveway. Pulling up to the garage, she left her car outside and raced to unlock her front door.

Stepping inside, her heart stopped.

"No," she cried. The curio cabinet lay overturned on the floor surrounded by her mother's precious teacup collection, which had broken into a thousand pieces.

Someone must have entered through the garage door she had failed to properly lock and smashed the only thing of any worth that had been her mother's. Kelly knew the vandal was gone. Whether it was Kyle Foglio or Lola Taylor or someone else didn't matter. All that mattered was that Kelly's heart was broken just like the porcelain keepsakes her mother had treasured.

Falling to her knees, Kelly dropped her head into her hands and cried loud, gut-wrenching sobs. Hot tears fell from her eyes as she relived the anguish of growing up poor and lonely, with a mother who loved a shiftless Cajun more than she loved her own child. The memory of that night of terror when her father had broken into their house returned.

Kelly had wanted to protect her mother but ended up making a mistake she would never stop regretting. If only she could recall all the details. Too much remained a terrible blur.

A knock sounded at her door. Kelly wiped her eyes and turned to see Sally Jacobs from Magnolia Gardens standing in her doorway. The nurse was middle-aged and slightly overweight, and her eyes were full of concern.

"I was heading to my car when I saw you drive by. I knew something was wrong." Sally entered the house and closed the door, her gaze falling on the broken china collection. "Your mother's teacups she always talked about."

Kelly sniffed. "Someone broke in."

"Oh, honey, I'm so sorry. You need to call the police."

But Kelly didn't have the energy to make another phone call. Instead, she stared at the broken porcelain. "Is...is anything salvageable?"

Sally stooped to pick up a small teacup edged in royal blue and Florentine gold. "Here's a hardy soul that made it."

Kelly tried to smile. "My mom's favorite. It belonged to her mother."

"Look, there's another one and a saucer." Sally reached for a number of pieces that had withstood the crash. "The thick carpet probably kept them from breaking."

Kelly folded the royal blue teacup against her chest and accepted a pack of tissues Sally pulled from her purse. The nurse rubbed Kelly's shoulder as she blew her nose and wiped her eyes.

"There's another reason I stopped by," Sally said. "Grace told me about Millie Taylor and her prescription drugs. She said you needed information about Dr. Kutter's pharmacy. Did Grace mention that my brother works there?"

Kelly shook her head.

"He's a pharmacy tech," Sally continued. "A few months ago, he realized something was going on and notified the authorities. He planned to quit his job, but they asked him to stay on and keep them informed."

"He's the whistle-blower?"

Sally nodded. "I told my brother you were concerned Millie's daughter-in-law might be over- or undermedicating her. I asked him to let me know if she came in to fill another prescription."

"That's information he shouldn't be giving out, Sally."

"Probably not, yet under the circumstances—" The nurse shrugged. "Besides, I told him how much Millie meant to me."

"And?"

"Lola Taylor came into the pharmacy today and filled a prescription for her mother-in-law."

"Oxycodone?"

Sally nodded.

Kelly thought of the land deal and the money Lola would make if Mildred was out of the way. "How easy would it be to overdose a frail, elderly woman with oxycodone?"

"If her medical condition was poor, it wouldn't take much to put her into respiratory arrest. Crush the pill and the rate of absorption increases."

Kelly's gut tightened. She had been worried about Lola selling Mildred's prescription drugs. Now she realized the daughter-in-law might want them for another reason.

Concerned for Mildred's safety, Kelly grabbed her purse and headed for the door. "Call the local cops. Ask for Tim Simpson and tell him what happened. I'm going to the farmhouse to check on Mildred. If Lola won't let me in, I'll call for police backup."

Kelly needed to ensure Mildred was okay, but as she drove away, she glanced at the passenger seat and thought about last night when Phil had been with her. More than anything, she wished he was with her now.

She tossed her hair and tried to shake off thoughts of Phil. She didn't want to think about him ever again.

Then she sighed. Who was she trying to fool?

* * *

As the farmhouse came into view, Kelly saw a pickup truck with a small travel trailer in tow, heading away along the back road. The cages with the gamecocks sat in the rear of the pickup.

Lola Taylor was at the wheel.

Kelly turned into the driveway as Lola and her entourage disappeared from sight. Knowing Mildred was probably in the house, Kelly hastened along the drive and screeched to a stop by the front door. She ran up the steps, grimacing as her right leg throbbed, reminding her of the injury she had sustained just a few nights ago.

Trying to ignore the pain, she pounded on the front door. "Mildred?"

Kelly grabbed the knob, but the door was locked, and just as when she and Phil had stopped by, curtains covered the front windows. Kelly raced as fast as her leg permitted to the rear of the house and thumped on that door. Jiggling the knob, she was relieved when the door opened.

"Mildred? It's Kelly McQueen from the CID. I'm coming in." Hand on her weapon, Kelly stepped into the quiet house. "Mildred?"

Silence was the only response she heard.

Racing to the back bedroom, Kelly flipped on the light and hastened to the woman's bedside. Her face was white and her breathing labored.

"Mildred, can you hear me?" She touched the woman's clammy cheek.

Pulling out her cell, Kelly called the EMTs. "Hurry."

Kelly rubbed Mildred's hand. "Lord, keep her breathing," she prayed as she waited for the sirens.

Once the ambulance pulled into the drive, Kelly motioned the medical team to the back bedroom. As they worked on

Mildred, Kelly stepped into the hallway and called her house. Sally answered.

"I'm sure Officer Simpson would like to talk to you," the nurse said.

"What in the world is going on?" Simpson demanded once he came on the line.

"I'm at the Taylor farmhouse. Lola left Mildred alone. She was going into respiratory distress, which could have been caused by an overdose of oxycodone. The EMTs are working on her now and plan to transport her to the Freemont Hospital shortly."

"How'd you get inside?"

"The kitchen door was open."

"Was it?"

Kelly hadn't expected anything negative from Simpson. "Do you think I'm lying?"

"No, of course not, but everything is happening a bit too quickly, in my opinion. You're out of bounds, Agent McQueen. Freemont isn't your jurisdiction. Do you understand?"

She understood that Simpson had become territorial.

"Don't do anything until I get there," he insisted. "I'll wrap things up here at your house in the next few minutes."

Kelly shook her head. She had expected more from Simpson.

Once she hung up, the EMT motioned her back into the bedroom. "Ms. Mildred's coming out of it, but she still needs medical attention. You got here just in time. Any longer and I'm afraid to say what would have happened." He pointed to Mildred. "She wants to talk to you."

Kelly stepped to the bed.

"Th...thank you," the old woman whispered. "Kyle?"

"Was he coming over to stay with you?"

Mildred nodded. "The…the pain." She shook her head ever so slightly. "I…I took two…pills from the nightstand."

Kelly spied the bottle of over-the-counter pain medication on the bedside table that Mildred must have taken but which had been too much for her fragile body to handle. Kelly gave the bottle to the EMTs and relayed what Mildred had done to help curb her pain, never realizing the additional medication would put her in serious distress.

Returning to Mildred, Kelly patted her hand. "Tell me about Lola. She left the house. Do you know where she's going?"

"M…map." The woman glanced into the hallway and the small bedroom that lay beyond. A laptop sat opened on a desk.

"Lola got a map off the computer?"

Mildred nodded.

"You're going to be okay," Kelly assured her. "The EMTs are taking you to the hospital."

"Ger…geriatric?"

"No, dear. You'll be in a good facility in town. You'll be taken care of there." With a sigh of relief, Mildred closed her eyes and fell asleep.

Lola had left her computer on, and Kelly printed off the last site she had visited on the web, which turned out to be a map of a rural area near the town of Montburg, Georgia, about eighty miles from Freemont.

Kelly waited until Mildred had been placed in the ambulance before she climbed into her car. Officer Simpson had yet to arrive, but Kelly didn't want to delay any longer.

Hopefully, Kelly would be able to find Lola and determine what she was involved in, which had to have a bearing on her husband's death. In less than twenty-four hours, Kelly needed to submit her report. Hopefully it would be enough time to determine what had happened on the live-fire range. Maybe then she could put the investigation and the company captain who had led his men in the fateful mission behind her.

But steering her car along the roadway, Kelly knew she would never be able to forget Jean Philippe Thibodeaux. The handsome Cajun had stolen her heart.

NINETEEN

Once the formal part of the Hail and Farewell concluded, Phil introduced Captain Sylvia Watters to the two lieutenants who had hovered closeby throughout the general's lengthy remarks.

"Sylvia called me a few hours ago when she arrived on post. She'll be working in the housing office."

The taller of the two men smiled. "A busy place with all the new personnel moving to Fort Rickman."

She smiled. "Phil was nice enough to give me directions to the Post Lodge. I don't actually sign in to post for another week."

"Then you'll be hailed next month." The eager lieutenant couldn't hide his interest.

"That's right. By then, my fiancé will have arrived. He's in Germany and slated to take over an infantry company here at Fort Rickman."

"Fiancé?" The lieutenant's face dropped.

Phil smiled, enjoying the moment. "Sylvia's engaged to an old friend of mine. He's six-three and runs a seven-minute mile." Both lieutenants quickly excused themselves and headed to the bar.

Sylvia and a newly married female captain starting talking about wedding dresses and honeymoons, which gave Phil an opportunity to track down Jamison. He found him on the far side of the room, standing next to a pretty brunette.

Phil sidled up to the CID agent.

Jamison didn't look happy with the interruption, especially when the woman excused herself and walked toward a group of senior officers and their wives.

"Who's she?" Phil asked.

Jamison pointed to one of the brigade commanders who smiled as she approached. "The colonel's daughter."

"She seemed to enjoy talking to you."

Jamison frowned. "Until you showed up."

"Sorry, buddy." Phil held up his hands. "But cut me a little slack, okay? It's been a long week."

"I hear you." Jamison looked over Phil's shoulder. "Where's Kelly?"

"That's what I wanted to ask you."

"She was here earlier. But you know Kel. She's not a party girl and probably decided to go home after the general finished with the hails and farewells. Although that redhead you're with may have scared her off." Jamison took a swig of his cola. "I thought you and Kelly were pretty tight."

"Tight?"

"Well—" Jamison shrugged. "Working together. Staying in close contact."

"Yeah, we were, but she's wrapping up the investigation and suddenly doesn't want me around."

Jamison raised his brow. "And that bothers you?"

"No." Phil shook his head. But the way Jamison continued to look at him, Phil knew the CID agent realized there was more going on than just the investigation.

Last night, Kelly had made it perfectly clear she didn't want anything to do with Phil, yet the way she returned his kisses had told him something else. Had that been the real

Kelly, without the defenses she put in place to protect her heart?

Phil would never know unless he went after her. But would she listen to him or would she continue to close him out of her life?

Heading north on the main highway, Kelly picked up her cell and left a message for Jamison, filling him in on what had happened.

"Call the Montburg police, and ask if they know of any cockfights in the area. If not, alert them that there may be one this weekend. I'll contact them when I get closer to town."

Kelly knew having the CID arrive uninvited could make the local police dig in their heels and demand more information before they reacted. A little advance warning sometimes opened doors that otherwise would remain closed.

Her cell chirped a few minutes later. Expecting to hear Jamison's voice, she was surprised when a cop from Vine Grove, Kentucky, introduced himself. "I got your message seeking information about Lola Taylor."

"Thanks for getting back to me."

"No problem. Lola's one of five girls. The oldest was a spitfire. Ran after a captain at Fort Knox."

"Probably the whole guy-in-a-uniform thing."

The cop chuckled. "Maybe. Lola was the baby and spoiled rotten. Always wanted more than she had money to buy. When she got married and moved away, most folks said good riddance. Funny thing. Her husband died unexpectedly a few years later. Right after he'd taken out an insurance policy."

"And she was the beneficiary?

"You guessed it."

"Did the insurance company investigate?"

"Not that I heard. Seems the amount of the policy wasn't

that significant by most standards today, although for Lola it probably whet her appetite for more. Of course, that's just my gut feeling."

"I understand completely. Do you know anything else about the family?"

"Only that the oldest daughter, who married the army captain, eventually divorced. She lives up north, although I'm not exactly sure where she and her son settled?"

"She's probably making a new life for herself."

"Maybe, although the kid used to come back to visit Lola and the other sisters. The boy had problems. Kind of a loner. Not what you think of as being an army guy's son."

Kelly wasn't sure what the police officer meant. "Because he had problems?"

"No. Tattoos. Body piercings."

She thought of Kyle and nodded. "I've got a kid like that down here in Georgia."

"Of course, fate piled up against this particular young man. His dad's in prison. You know what they say about the apple not falling—"

"Far from the tree." Kelly's neck tingled. "Did you get the kid's name?"

"I wrote it down." Kelly waited as he searched through his notes. "Here it is. Last name's Filio."

Kelly pushed the phone closer to her ear. "Could it be Foglio? Kyle Foglio?"

The cop chuckled. "Sorry. Sometimes I can't read my own writing." He laughed again. "Yeah, that's it. Lola's nephew's name is Kyle Foglio."

After dropping Sylvia off at the Post Lodge, Phil left Fort Rickman and headed north on the Freemont Road. Passing Magnolia Gardens, his heart kicked up a notch when he spied a cop car in Kelly's driveway.

Jamming on the brakes, he yanked his keys from the ignition and raced for the front door. His breath came in short gasps, and his heart felt like it was wedged in his throat. *Please, Lord, let Kelly be all right.*

He jiggled the knob. When it failed to open, he pounded on the door. "Kelly? Open up. It's Phil."

His knock was answered by a young cop with a thick neck and square face. Before he could say anything, Phil pushed past the officer.

"What happened? Is she hurt?" His eyes searched the living area. "Kelly?"

Phil's gaze fell on the curio cabinet and broken porcelain.

"Did someone break in?" He raised his voice, frantic that Kelly had been attacked. "Is she at the hospital?"

Simpson stepped from the kitchen and put a firm hand on Phil's shoulder.

He didn't need the cop's calming touch. He wanted to know about Kelly. "Tell me, where she is? Was she hurt?"

"Settle down, Captain. She's fine. In fact, she may have saved Mildred Taylor's life. Luckily the back door of the Taylor home was unlocked. Guess Ms. Mildred was having breathing problems. The EMTs said if Kelly hadn't arrived when she did, the old woman might not still be with us. As it was, they fixed her up and transported her to the hospital in town."

"Kelly's okay?"

"She's fine."

Relief swept over Phil, causing his knees to weaken for a second and his heart to jerk back into his chest. He felt drained and elated at the same time.

He pointed to the broken porcelain. "So who did the damage?"

"That's what we're trying to determine. Could be that Foglio kid. The garage door was pried open."

"What about the entrance to the kitchen? It should have held."

"Seems Agent McQueen left her house in a hurry this morning and forgot to flip the lock."

"Was anything taken?"

"Not that we can tell. Kelly will have to do a thorough search once she gets home."

"Do you expect her soon?"

"More than likely. I just got back from checking out the farmhouse. Found something suspicious in the barn. I've got a team out there now, digging up the soil, trying to find the body of an old codger who belongs to a wallet we uncovered."

"Catfish Ryan?"

"Exactly. Mildred's in the hospital, holding her own. I've got someone questioning her, but I doubt she's involved."

"What about the deserted trailer? Kelly might have gone after Kyle Foglio."

"A couple officers are checking that out, as well. Kelly should turn up any minute now. I'll call you when she does."

Phil left with a sick feeling in his gut. Kelly was in even more danger now that someone had broken into her house. Knowing how stubborn she was about not allowing the perpetrator to control her life, she would probably insist on staying at her own house tonight. Phil couldn't let that happen.

Once he was in his truck, he called her cell and was relieved when she answered.

"Kelly, it's me. Look, I'm sorry about last night."

"I told you it's okay, Phil." He could barely hear her voice with the hum of her car engine in the background.

"No, really, I was a jerk. You've got a lot on your shoulders with the investigation. I never meant to influence you in any way."

When she didn't respond, he tried another tactic. "I

wanted to introduce you to Sylvia Watters at the club to-night."

"The redhead?"

"So you did see her? Sylvia arrived on post this afternoon. I invited her to the Hail and Farewell."

"She…she's very pretty."

Did he detect a bit of jealousy? Phil almost smiled. Maybe there was hope for him after all. "She's engaged to the best friend a guy could have."

"Oh?" Kelly's voice carried a bit more interest.

"Sylvia is staying at the Post Lodge. You need to get a room there, at least until Kyle Foglio is found and arrested."

"Is that all you wanted to tell me, Phil?"

He let out a deep breath. No, there was so much more he wanted to say about all the crazy feelings swelling up within him that had to do with home and family and being with Kelly for the rest of his life. But now wasn't the time. Now he had to focus on her safety.

"You've got to be careful, Kelly, until this investigation is over."

"Is the investigation all you're worried about?"

He swallowed hard. "I'm worried about you. I was at your house tonight. When I saw what happened, my stomach tied up in knots—"

The background noise ceased. "Kelly?"

He looked down at his phone. CALL DISCONNECTED.

His heart plummeted. Phil redialed and got her voice mail. Was Kelly out of range or had she hung up and turned off her phone?

The first question he should have asked her was "Where are you?" Then he would have known how to find her. Instead he had talked about the investigation. Although important, his main concern was for Kelly. More than anything, he wanted to wrap her in his arms and keep her safe.

TWENTY

Twenty miles south of Montburg, Kelly was still thinking about Phil's disconnected phone call. She wished he would have tried her again, although as sporadic as cell service was in this part of rural Georgia perhaps he couldn't get through. Right now she needed to distance herself from him and focus instead on finding Lola.

Excited though she had been when her cell had rung and Kelly had seen Phil's name on the caller ID, her hopes had been dashed when he turned the conversation back to the investigation. The outcome was the only thing that mattered to him.

At least she now knew the redhead wasn't Phil's girlfriend, but then, neither was Kelly.

Letting out a groan, she combed her fingers through her hair. "When will I ever learn?"

Shaking off her frustration, she glanced at her near-empty fuel tank and pulled into a service station that sat at the intersection of the highway and a narrow two-lane road. As she pumped fuel, she watched the steady flow of traffic, mainly travel trailers and pickups that turned onto the side road. The constant flow of vehicles heading up the mountain stirred her curiosity.

"Where's that two-lane head?" she asked the clerk when she went inside to pay.

He shrugged. "A few campsites are nestled up in the hills. We usually see outdoors enthusiasts in the warmer months. I'm not sure what's going on this weekend. One of the guys buying gas an hour or so ago wanted to cash a check. He said he planned to double his money this weekend."

"Oh?" Kelly raised her brow with interest. "The local cops ever come out this way?"

The clerk smiled. "You're not from around here, are you, lady? Otherwise you'd know Montburg hasn't had a police force for the last four years. We rely on the county sheriff, or always did. He passed away six weeks ago. The deputy sheriff retired shortly before that, so right now, we're without law enforcement. 'Course there's always Pine Gate Landing. They've got a chief of police and a few officers on duty most days."

"How far away is Pine Gate Landing?"

The guy rubbed his chin. "Twenty miles to Montburg and another twenty to Pine Gate Landing, so a total of forty miles, give or take."

"Do you have the number to their police department?"

"Sure do." He scratched the digits on a piece of paper and handed it to her. "Problem is there's no way to contact them from here. Storm knocked out my landline, and the hills around here interfere with cell reception. As I tell folks, if you need the police, keep driving east."

At this point, Kelly didn't want to go forty miles out of her way just to tell the local cops about an influx of travel trailers that may have no bearing on finding Lola. Kelly planned to follow the flow of traffic and see where it led her. If she was lucky, she might discover the widow and her roosters. With concrete information about Lola's whereabouts, she could then go to the police and expect to get their attention.

Not that Kelly would try to be a hero before she knew

what was really going on. Instead, she'd take a quick look around the mountain campsite and assess whether she needed to notify the local authorities, even if it meant driving to Pine Gate Landing. At least then she'd have proof that something was going down.

Her jacket was in the car, but Kelly didn't want the CID logo on the front to draw attention to herself or her job, so she pulled a hooded sweatshirt and a pair of sunglasses off the nearby merchandise racks. She paid cash for the items and hurried back to the car.

Kelly followed the road through the forest and up the hill. Lowering her speed, she shoved her gear into Low to ease the strain on her engine. The last thing she wanted was car trouble in the middle of nowhere.

Eventually, the road leveled off and angled into a campsite with picnic tables and trash receptacles where at least thirty trailers had parked in a circle. Kelly pulled off the road near a cluster of pines and studied the vehicles, searching for Lola Taylor's trailer and pickup.

She checked her cell, but as the service station attendant had indicated, coverage was down. She wanted to let Jamison know where she was and ask him to send backup. He knew she had headed to Montburg but wouldn't realize she had turned off the main road to town.

Kelly also wanted to talk to Phil again. But as much as she wanted to hear his voice, what would she say? You're always on my mind and I need you in my life? Wasn't that what her mother would have done?

Kelly wouldn't follow in her mother's footsteps no matter how much she longed to be with Phil again.

Phil stormed into his headquarters, needing something to occupy his mind other than wondering where Kelly was and whether she would ever answer his phone calls again.

The first sergeant looked up as he entered. "Rough afternoon, sir?"

"What gave you that idea?"

The sergeant shrugged. "Could be the scowl you're wearing or the door you slammed on the way in here, or the way you're stamping your boots like you want to kick someone in the hind end."

"Is it that obvious?"

"Only to someone who knows you. After a year together in Afghanistan, I can read you, sir."

"I just need some time alone to catch up on paperwork."

"Roger that, sir."

Phil started into his office and then turned back to the sergeant. "What are you doing here this late on a Friday?"

"Waiting for the Mrs. She had to pick up our daughter from an after-school activity." He glanced at his watch. "I expect them here any minute."

"Enjoy the weekend," Phil mumbled as he entered his office. He looked at the stack of papers in his inbox, knowing an equal number of emails required his attention. As much as he tried, he couldn't keep his mind on anything except Kelly.

Riffling through the papers on his desk, Phil found the master list for the live-fire demonstration. He glanced over the names, searching for some connection with the Foglio kid.

A woman's voice sounded outside his office, followed by a knock at his door. "Evening, Captain." Mrs. Meyers stepped inside, holding a plate of cookies. The first sergeant's wife was pretty, with curly brown hair and green eyes that twinkled when she smiled.

"You guys have been having a hard time with the investigation. I thought a batch of chocolate chip cookies might lift your sprits."

Phil's mood instantly took a turn for the better. "Mrs. Meyers, your husband is a lucky man."

She laughed, enjoying the flattery, and placed the plate on his desk. "I keep telling him that, but I'm not sure he always agrees."

Phil reached for a cookie and closed his eyes as he bit into the still warm chocolate chips. "Things are starting to look up already."

Rounding his desk to give her a hug of thanks, his eyes glanced once again at the invitation list. "Mrs. Meyers, when you were at the live-fire demonstration, did you happen to see a teenage boy—"

She held up her hand. "I couldn't make it at the last minute. Our daughter had planned to go with me so I told her to invite one of her friends. She took a young man she's been dating."

Phil stopped chewing.

Mrs. Meyers glanced from Phil to her husband, who now stood in the doorway. "I hope that was okay. I didn't call battalion headquarters to tell them about the change."

Phil stepped closer. "No, no. That was fine. Not a problem. Tell me about this young man."

Mrs. Meyers looked embarrassed. "She met him last year. His dad lived in the Hunter Housing Area on post. His parents are divorced so he spends most of the year up north with his mom. He came down for a few days." Mrs. Meyers shrugged. "I thought it would be okay if he took my spot."

"What's your daughter's full name?"

"Marie Madison, but why—"

"And her boyfriend is Kyle Foglio?"

Her eyes opened in surprise. "Why, yes. Do you know him?"

Phil didn't want to alarm Mrs. Meyers, but he doubted

whether she or her husband realized their daughter might be in danger.

"Would you mind if I talk to your daughter?" Phil asked the first sergeant. "I'd like to ask her a few questions."

"She's in the car outside," Mrs. Meyers said. The first sergeant left the office and returned with a pretty girl in tow. Marie had long brown hair and big eyes. She looked quizzically from her parents to Phil.

He would have a talk with the first sergeant later about keeping his daughter away from Kyle, but right now, Phil needed answers. He explained briefly that Kyle could be involved in something criminal.

"Oh, no," Mrs. Meyers moaned.

Phil turned to the girl. "When was the last time you saw Kyle?"

"A couple days ago. We met in town."

"Did he tell you where he was staying?"

"No, sir." Her response had come too quickly, and the hint of pink that colored her cheeks told more than her answer.

Phil glanced at the first sergeant, who understood the silent message Phil was trying to send.

"Marie Madison, you tell the truth to the captain."

She lowered her gaze and tapped her foot against the floor. When she looked up, her eyes were wide and the color had left her cheeks. "Actually he's been camping in the woods. At first, he stayed in an old trailer, but he said people kept stopping by to check it out. He was afraid he'd be sent back to his mother if they found him there."

"Did you see any cuts or scratches on his arms?"

She nodded. "He was helping his Aunt Lola with her roosters."

"His aunt?"

Madison nodded. "His mom doesn't want him around. She's got a job and works nights. Kyle's always alone. When he asks her to find a new job so they can be together after school, she gets mad. When she threw him out of the house this time, he came to see Lola."

Whether that was true or something Kyle had made up to garner sympathy from Marie was hard to say. "Why doesn't Kyle stay with his aunt?"

"He doesn't like her boyfriend."

"You mean her husband?"

The girl shook her head. "No, the husband was nice to Kyle."

Phil's neck tingled. "Did he mention the boyfriend's name?"

"Only that he was in the army."

"Sir," the first sergeant stepped forward. "Does this have anything to do with Corporal Taylor's death?"

"That's what I'm trying to find out. Did Kyle ever mention a CID agent named Kelly McQueen?"

Marie shook her head. "No, sir."

"If you hear from Kyle, would you let him know I'd like to talk to him?"

"Is he in trouble?"

Phil didn't want to lie to the teen. "He'll be in more trouble if he doesn't come forward. You let your dad know if Kyle contacts you."

Glancing up at the sergeant he added, "Call me if he comes around. I need to talk to him, and the local authorities will want to, as well."

"I don't want him to get hurt," Marie said.

"Of course you don't. The best thing is for Kyle to be truthful, just as you have been."

The first sergeant walked his wife and daughter to their car while Phil called Officer Simpson and relayed what he had learned about Kyle and Lola Taylor.

He also left a message for Jamison. "I'm heading back to

Freemont to search for Kelly. I'll stop at her house in case she returned home. When I find her, I'll bring her back to post. With Kyle Foglio still on the loose, it's too dangerous for Kelly to stay at her house tonight, even though she thinks she's safe there."

The traffic to get off post had backed up and cars were inching past the main gate. Phil drummed his fingers on the steering wheel and stared ahead, his mind on what Marie had revealed.

Kelly may have been right about Lola after all. Cockfighting was a nasty business, and the betting and rowdy gatherings spelled trouble and were against the law. Lola could be making a little extra money on the side.

Had her husband been involved? Or her boyfriend?

He thought back to Lola's reticence the night of her husband's death. If she had been expecting someone, no wonder she had hurried them out of the house.

When Phil had gone back later, he'd seen the light-colored pickup with the unit decal on the rear bumper and had thought one of the wives was comforting the grieving widow.

He shook his head in disgust. More than likely, Lola was being comforted by the boyfriend. Phil's neck tingled. If the boyfriend was in the company, he had a motive for killing Corporal Taylor.

Irritated by the traffic, Phil stretched to determine what the holdup was. His gaze fell on a pickup truck three vehicles ahead of him.

He couldn't see the driver because of the tinted windows, but the pickup was light beige with big tires and spiked spokes. A Ford 4x4 Dually Extended Cab with Sprewell rims, a souped-up special model, probably one of a kind, at least in this area. But what caught his eye was the unit decal on the right rear bumper. The truck was identical to the one that had visited Lola's farmhouse the night of the live-fire mission.

The 4x4 left post and headed north along the Freemont Road. Phil followed at a distance. He wanted to see where the truck went and who was behind the wheel. Then he'd have information Kelly would want for her investigation. Maybe then, she'd answer his call.

TWENTY-ONE

Kelly slipped into the sweatshirt and pulled the hood up around her head. Luckily, the baggy fleece covered the gun on her hip. The sun was low on the horizon but still shining, which gave her a reason to wear the sunglasses.

Some of the people set up campsites while a few men cleared leaves and debris from the center area and dug a shallow pit. Lawn chairs and coolers were positioned nearby, probably in anticipation of whatever would occur later in the evening.

The crowd was a rough mix of big burly guys in baseball caps and flannel shirts and lean, wiry dudes with weather-worn faces and narrow eyes. Kelly noted a few cages on the backside of the clearing. Each contained a gamecock.

She spied Lola's pickup and camper in the rear of the campsite near the wooded area. As she watched, Lola came out of the trailer and was approached by three men, all over six feet tall with wide torsos and thick necks. They were dressed in flannel shirts, jeans and work boots with baseball caps tugged low over their foreheads.

Pulling out her phone, Kelly activated the camera and snapped pictures of the group. Once she was in range, she would send the photos to the local authorities to see if they could identify the men. She also wanted the photos of Lola

Taylor as proof that Corporal Taylor's widow was doing more than grieving for her husband.

Lola passed a small plastic bag to the one of the men. He drew money from his wallet and shoved a wad of bills into her hands, which Kelly caught on the video setting of her phone.

Probably the oxycodone prescribed for Mildred.

But Kelly had to be sure.

She sidled up to a man who poured charcoal into his portable grill. "What time's dinner?"

He chuckled, a flicker of interest in his gaze. "As soon as the wife arrives with the beer and burgers."

Subtle way to let her know he was married. Kelly nodded toward Lola and her friends. "Anything going on around here?"

He picked up on her inference. "Angel dust, Barbies, jay smoke or coke?"

"What about O.C.'s?"

The guy threw a match on the coals, which ignited into a blaze. Kelly held her breath. Maybe she'd said too much.

Finally, he stepped back from the flames, but his eyes remained on his grill. "See Lola. She's got oxycodone. People say it's good. Not that I'd know."

"Who are her friends?" Kelly fixed her gaze on the three men still talking to Lola.

"The biggest guy's Jake. He's a mean varmint. Better to stay away from him. He and the other two big boys run the fights. Lola's part of the operation. Her husband was as well, but from what I hear, he passed on a few days ago."

"She doesn't look too upset."

He eyed Lola and shrugged. "You want me to introduce you?"

She shook her head. "I think we've already met."

Hearing the crunch of tires over the dead leaves, Kelly

turned as a minivan braked to a stop. A woman with bleached hair and raised brows stared at Kelly. The look on her face said Don't Mess With My Man.

"Appreciate your help." Kelly turned and walked into the growing crowd of people, hoping to distance herself from the jealous wife.

The stranger with the grill had provided enough information for Kelly to know her gut feeling was right on target. As much as she wanted to arrest Lola and her friends, doing so at this point would be foolish.

Instead, Kelly needed to head back down the hill to Pine Gate Landing. Hopefully, the police chief would be interested in what was happening at the remote campsite.

She cut through the trailers to where she had parked her Corolla. Opening the driver's door, Kelly tossed her cell on the consul and started to slide onto the seat. The sound of footsteps caused her to turn. One of the boys in flannel stood next to Lola Taylor.

"Agent McQueen, what brings you to this neck of the woods?" the not-so-grieving widow asked.

Kelly dropped her keys and reached for her gun. Before she could withdraw her weapon, a second man put his arm around her throat.

Kelly dug her fingernails into his flesh, needing to break his hold. She couldn't breath.

Lola opened her mouth and laughed, but Kelly couldn't hear anything except the roar in her ears.

She kicked her feet and attempted to free herself.

The pressure around her neck increased until Lola's face disappeared. Kelly gasped for air and everything went black.

Phil followed the extended-cab pickup, hanging back far enough not to be seen. At least that's what he hoped. Maybe he was crazy, but Kelly had talked about gut feelings she needed to follow, which was exactly what Phil was doing. If she wasn't interested in talking to him, then his only recourse was to determine who had stopped by the Taylor farmhouse the night the corporal had died.

He called Jamison and left a message, describing the truck and the road he was on. Before he hung up, Phil added, "If you see Kelly, tell her to call me."

When Phil disconnected, he was overcome with frustration. More than likely he was on a wild goose chase, but he'd do anything to get to the bottom of the investigation and to be able to talk to Kelly again.

TWENTY-TWO

Kelly moaned. Her head throbbed as she floated in and out of consciousness. Someone was talking. A male voice.

"We've got to get rid of her, Lola."

"Later, Jake."

"I told you to be careful. Then that so-called boyfriend of yours killed Rick."

"He had the opportunity and took it, which works to our advantage. Rick found out I was selling his mother's drugs and was ready to turn me in."

"So you conned that army guy into killing him?"

She chuckled. "I mentioned the insurance and the sweet deal from the housing developer. When the stupid private handed him a rifle, he thought it was fate."

"Fate? More like he wants to have you to himself, Lola."

"Now, Jake, you're not getting jealous, are you?"

"You know how I feel, baby."

"And I've told you we need to bide our time."

"I can get rid of him, then it'll just be you and me."

"First, we have to take care of the agent."

"No one will find her when I get finished with her."

Kelly blinked her eyes open. Was she dreaming or had she really heard voices?

The muscles in her neck screamed for attention and her

throat was dry as cardboard. She needed water and a good massage.

At least she wasn't dead. Her last thought before she'd blacked out had been about making right with the Lord. Evidently He'd given her a second chance.

Her hands were tied in front of her, and she was lying on a bed with rumpled sheets and a flowered comforter. She glanced at knotty pine paneling in the small travel trailer and the window directly above her head.

The voices came again. "Where's that oxycodone?"

"You can't mix pills, Jake. You've had enough."

"Come on, baby."

From the sounds in the next room, Lola and Jake would be occupied for a while.

Easing off the bed, Kelly stood. Her head pounded, and her blood pressure took a dive. She leaned against the wall until her equilibrium stabilized.

The window was open, letting in fresh air that helped to clear her foggy head. If she could get outside, she'd be able to escape.

Kelly pushed both hands against the screen until it jiggled free and fell noisily to the ground. She held her breath. Lola's playful laughter sent a wave of relief coursing through Kelly.

She crawled onto the bed and glanced outside into the night. Drop and roll might work. If only her hands were free. Kelly lifted one leg and then the other, holding on to the upper window casing for support as she shimmied her trunk through the narrow opening.

"Augh!" She landed on her bad leg, which crumpled beneath her. Her hands hit the hard Georgia clay, and she gasped as pain jarred her to the core.

Rising from the dirt, Kelly steadied herself against the side of the trailer, unsure if her leg would hold. Gingerly, she took one step and then another.

A sharp piece of metal scraped her hand. Looking down, she saw the siding had pulled away from the edge of the trailer.

A sense of triumph swept over her. Someone's fender bender would provide a way to cut the rope that held her bound. Kelly rubbed the hemp back and forth over the sharp edge until it split in two, freeing her hands. Massaging her wrists, she heard a swell of voices and peered around the corner of the trailer, surprised by the number of people who had gathered around the makeshift pit.

Some stood, while others lounged in folding chairs. Amber bottles were passed from mouth to mouth, and a growing pile of discarded beer cans littered the ground. The bright lights from a few pickups illuminated the pit area where two gamecocks flew at each other. Their sharp talons and the knife gaffs attached to their legs drew blood. The crowd egged the cocks on with their hoots and catcalls. Money exchanged hands as bets were placed on which bird would survive the fight to the death.

Pulling the hood of the sweatshirt around her face, Kelly wove her way around the back of the onlookers. She had dropped her car keys on the floorboard of her Corolla when she had reached for her gun earlier. If she could find the keys, she'd be able to drive to Pine Gate Landing and notify the authorities.

Before she cleared the throng of people, a hand clamped down on her arm.

"Where do you think you're going?"

She turned, recognizing the voice.

"Kyle Foglio, I knew you were involved."

The souped-up pickup turned onto a side road that wove in front of a gas station and then headed into a densely forested, hilly area. Phil was beginning to think the guy had spotted him and was setting him up for an ambush.

Ready to turn around, Phil changed his mind when the pickup pulled into a clearing where trucks and travel trailers circled a campsite. The center of the area was lit by the headlights of a number of vehicles and revealed a crowd of people who concentrated their attention on the center of the ring.

Phil's stomach dropped. From the raucous sounds of the crowd, he had a hunch it involved gamecocks and illegal betting.

The beige pickup came to a stop. Phil parked farther back in a thickly wooded area and watched from afar as the driver stepped from the truck, still in uniform, just as Phil was.

Reaching into his glove compartment, he pulled out his binoculars, raised them to his eyes and whistled. "How about that?"

As he watched, Staff Sergeant Greg Gates—Private Stanley's squad leader—met up with a woman on the steps of a distant trailer. Phil adjusted the oculars until Lola Taylor came into view. From the way Gates draped his arm around her shoulder, more than just friendship was involved.

Phil focused on the crowd to see if he recognized anyone else. A cold chill swept over him. A young kid with tattoos and a number of piercings stood in the midst of the throng.

Kyle Foglio?

In his hands, he held a gun aimed at Kelly.

Kelly tried to jerk her arm free from Kyle's hold, but he had brandished her own Sig Sauer and shoved it into her side.

"Did Lola give you my gun? You've been working with her, haven't you, Kyle?"

"She's helping me."

"Helping you get into trouble that could send you to jail for life. Did Lola tell you to break into my garage?"

"That was Sergeant Gates. His opener activated your garage the night my uncle died. He wanted to scare you so you couldn't do your job."

"Lola plans to kill me, Kyle. That makes you an accomplice to murder."

"I don't believe you." He pushed her toward Lola's trailer, his fingers digging into her arm.

Spying the man with the grill and his possessive wife, Kelly knew they might be her only chance to survive. She threw her full weight against Kyle's chest, jerked her arm free and stumbled into the crowd.

Pushing deeper into the mass of people, Kelly glanced at the trailer, surprised to see Staff Sergeant Gates standing next to Lola. No coincidence there. The sergeant had to be involved with the widow and with her husband's death, as well.

Lola's eyes widened as she realized the agent was on the loose. "Stop her!" Gates pulled a .38 special from his waistband and disappeared into the crowd.

Approaching the man and his wife, Kelly grabbed both their hands. "I'm an army CID agent. Lola Taylor plans to kill me. I need your help."

The woman started to say something, but the husband pushed her aside. He grabbed Kelly's shoulders, spun her around with a dizzying effect and shoved her toward the center of the throng. "Look what I've got for you, Lola."

Kelly had made a terrible mistake. Her stomach roiled and bile climbed up her throat. Weak as she was, she dug in her heels and tried to free herself from his hold.

All around her, the angry mob raised their fists and jeered. Hands reached for her. Someone struck her face. She gasped, unable to understand their frenzy. They poked and prodded her as the man continued to push her forward.

"No," she demanded.

With one violent thrust, he shoved her into the pit. Her leg buckled. She went down on one knee.

The cocks swirled around her. She put her arm over her eyes to protect herself from the knives attached to the game-cocks' legs.

Lola broke through the crowd and stood on the sidelines. "Place your bets, ladies and gentlemen. Who's going to win this fight, the cocks or the woman?" Her laughter floated over the taunts of the mob.

The birds flew at Kelly. Their wings flapped the air while their sharp talons and the metal gaffs cut into her flesh. Blood ran along her neck and down her arms. Her eyes burned, and she coughed at the dirt raised from the wild birds and the even wilder crowd.

In a final flurry of feathers, the birds clawed at Kelly's back and plucked at her hair.

"Dear God, help me," she screamed.

TWENTY-THREE

Phil shoved his way through the crowd like a madman. He had to get to Kelly. Hands held him back, but he fought them off.

"Kelly," he cried, seeing the birds attack. Blood spattered her hair and clothing.

He lunged forward, jumped into the pit and swatted the fighting cocks away from her bleeding body. Pulling her protectively into his arms, he turned to fight off the crowd that booed and hissed around them.

"Back off!" Phil raised his voice. "She's with the CID. Military law enforcement. You're all under arrest."

"Don't listen to him," Lola shouted from the sidelines. She waved her hands with frustration as the crazed crowd suddenly quieted. People backed away from the pit. Others turned and scrambled to their cars. "Wait. Don't leave."

Jake and his two buddies came out of the trailer. "What the—"

Seeing an opening in the crowd, Phil pointed to the woods. "Run, Kelly. I'll hold them off."

She clung to him. "Not without you."

Gates came up behind Phil and shoved a revolver in his back.

"Go," Phil insisted, urging her forward.

Kelly's knee buckled and she stumbled. Hands grabbed her. She turned to see Kyle.

Lashing out at him, she tried to get free, but he wrapped his arm around her neck and held the Sig Sauer to her head. "Don't make me hurt you."

Phil tensed, ready to lunge. Even if Gates fired, Phil might be able to get to Kelly in time.

"No you don't, Captain." The sergeant slammed the revolver against the side of Phil's neck. He groaned and doubled over.

Twisting Phil's hands behind his back, Gates forced him upright. "I wouldn't do anything foolish, Captain, if I were you."

"Phil," Kelly gasped.

He blinked until she came into focus. Her hands gripped the teen's arm, which was around her neck, trying to keep him from tightening his hold.

Although her eyes were wide with fear, her voice was calm. "You're not a killer, Kyle."

"My dad is and people say I'm just like him." The teen shook his head. "Besides, I...I can't trust you."

"Then listen to me." Phil raised his voice. Unable to break free from Gates's hold, his eyes flicked between Kyle and the three big guys who were fiddling with something at the side of the pit. "My dad went to jail, Kyle. He made a mistake that cost two people their lives. I'm his son, but that doesn't make me a bad person. You can be a better man than your father."

Hearing Phil's comments, Lola shook her head. "Don't listen to him, Kyle."

Jake glanced up from what he was doing. The brute's eyes were dilated, and a manic sneer spread across his wide face as he stared at Phil. "Because of you, we're gonna lose a lot of money this weekend, Captain. The way the boys and I figure, you owe us."

Lola wrinkled her brow. "What are you doing, Jake?"

"We're going to have a fight to the death, baby. Only it won't be the cocks that die." He held up his mammoth hands. On each finger, he had strapped a two-inch gaff, the blades razor-sharp.

Tightening his hold on Phil, Gates chuckled. "We'll let Jake have a little fun with you, Captain Thibodeaux, before we kill you and the agent."

Phil's eyes focused on Kelly. The color had drained from her face, and blood matted her hair and clothing. He had to protect her. *Lord, I need help.*

"You'll never get away with this, Gates."

"Sure we will, Captain. No one will ever find your bodies."

"What about all the people watching the cockfight? Someone will talk."

"No, sir. They'll be too afraid for their own sakes."

As Phil looked around, he realized Gates might be right. Many of the people had already fled. Even if someone called the police, they wouldn't get here in time.

Kelly's heart lodged in her throat. She had to do something. "Give me the gun, Kyle. I'll help you get out of this rap."

The two thugs stepped into the pit and circled around the sergeant.

"You know what I don't like?" Jake stood on the sidelines and flexed his fingers.

The sergeant swallowed hard and nervously eyed Jake and then the men who approached him from each side.

Kelly's pulse accelerated. Phil was in the middle of a

bunch of lunatics vying to get the upper hand. *Dear God, protect him.*

"I don't like someone else messing with my woman," Jake sneered.

Gates's face paled. He glared at Lola.

She laughed nervously and shrugged. "I had to tell him."

Jake flicked his wrist at the taller of his two friends and pointed to the sergeant. "Take care of that weasel."

The tall one stepped closer. "Drop the gun, Sarge."

Gates eased his hold on Phil and took a step back. "Let's be calm, boys. Remember, I'm the one with the weapon.

Glancing over his shoulder, Gates eyed the second man, who was moving closer. Raising the .38, Gates took aim and fired.

The second guy clutched his chest. Blood covered his flannel shirt. He staggered backward to the edge of the pit and crumpled to the ground.

Phil grabbed Gates's arm and wrestled for the gun. The thug kicked and his boot caught Phil's chin, forcing him to his knees. He rolled clear as Gates and the tall guy fought for control of the .38. Two more rounds exploded from the revolver.

Lola screamed.

The tall guy gained control of the weapon and fired. Gates's eyes flared. The thug fired again and again until the sergeant collapsed in the dirt.

Six rounds spent. The cylinder of the .38 was empty, although Kelly doubted Jake or his friend had done the math.

"Now that we've taken care of that problem, let's see what we can do about you, Captain." Jake jumped into the pit and lunged at Phil.

He dodged the first strike, but the tall guy with the gun jammed the weapon in his waistband and caught Phil in a bear hug, pinning his arms behind his back. From the smirk on his face, the guy in flannel appeared to be enjoying himself.

Jake danced closer and jabbed at Phil's chest.

He struggled to free himself. "You're a coward, Jake."

"No one ever said I had to fight fair, Captain."

Phil kicked, blocking Jake's hand, which only enraged the brute more. He swiped at Phil's chest. The gaffs ripped at his uniform and drew blood.

"Kyle, don't you understand, they're going to kill him." Kelly's pulse raced. "Give me the gun."

The teen looked confused.

She pushed on. "That's what they did to you the night I saw you on the road, wasn't it, Kyle?"

He nodded. "They…they were drugged up and wanted to show me what a cockfight was like."

Jake taunted Phil, the sharp gaffs inches from his face. With his arms pinned back, Phil didn't have a chance.

Kelly's voice was soft but firm. "Kyle—"

He relaxed his hold. The Sig Sauer slipped from his hand into hers.

One shot. If she missed the brute, she'd hit Phil.

If she didn't fire, he'd be dead in seconds.

"Jake?"

Kelly's voice caused Jake to glance at her over his shoulder. His eyes were on fire with rage and drugs.

"Stop or I'll shoot," she ordered.

Turning back to Phil, Jake raised his hands to strike. "I'm gonna kill you," he screamed, just as her father had screamed at her so long ago.

Kelly aimed her Sig Sauer and fired.

TWENTY-FOUR

The last thug still standing fired back at Kelly. Too late, he realized the revolver was out of ammo. Phil took him down and jammed his face into the dirt.

Kelly ordered Kyle and Lola to lie down on the ground with their hands clasped behind their heads. "Don't move or I'll shoot."

Sirens sounded in the distance. Within minutes, a string of police cars turned into the clearing.

"Law enforcement. Drop your weapons."

At the sound of Jamison's voice, gratitude swept over Kelly. Cops swarmed the campsite and took the guilty into custody.

Suddenly light-headed, Kelly collapsed onto the nearby picnic table. Phil was at her side.

"I'm okay," she assured him. "What about you?"

Blood soaked the front of his uniform and his chest and arms were cut, but his face and eyes were clear.

"Nothing a little tape can't fix." He smiled and she sighed with relief.

The EMTs approached them. "Let's get you cleaned up, ma'am."

Kelly shook her head. "I'm okay. Take care of the others first."

"Gates is dead, ma'am. Along with one of the big boys in flannel."

"What about Jake?"

"He's still breathing. Nice shot, by the way."

Jamison worked with the local authorities to load Lola, Kyle, Jake and the surviving thug into the squad cars while the EMTs bandaged first Kelly's wounds and then Phil's. When the medics moved on, Jamison joined them at the picnic table.

"Took you long enough to get here," she teased.

Jamison smiled, but his eyes were serious. "I was worried, Kel. We circled around Montburg for over an hour but didn't know where to look. Luckily, the attendant at the local service station mentioned a petite blonde with blue eyes who stopped for gas and information. About that time, a stream of travel trailers and pickups screeched onto the main road. Only one reason I could think of that so many people would be running scared."

"We owe you," Phil said.

"Yeah? Well, between the voice mails you two left, I was able to piece together the general vicinity of where you were headed. That made all the difference."

Kelly raised her brow. "Speaking of voice mail, where were you earlier?"

The usually put-together CID agent averted his gaze and shrugged. "I had a date after the Hail and Farewell."

Phil smiled knowingly. "The colonel's daughter?"

Jamison made up an excuse about needing to talk to the Pine Gate Landing chief of police and excused himself without answering Phil's question.

"Looks like Jamison may be in love." Kelly laughed, but when she looked at Phil, she realized he might be, as well.

She needed to clear the air about her past before they went any farther. Phil deserved to know the whole truth.

She sat silently for a long moment before she spoke. "I…I never talk about the night my father came after my mother. She had bought a gun for protection and kept it in the kitchen. My dad broke into the house. He had a knife and was cutting her."

Kelly bit her lip. "I blocked out the rest of what happened, but when Jake turned on you, it all came back."

The compassion she saw in Phil's gaze helped her find the courage to go on. "I was fifteen and had never handled a firearm before that night, but I had to help my mom. I opened the kitchen drawer and grabbed the gun—"

Pulling in a deep breath, Kelly continued, "My mother told the police it was self-defense, but I wasn't sure whether she was telling the truth or trying to save her daughter from going to jail."

Kelly attempted to smile, but her lips quivered. Phil reached for her hand. "And now you know the truth?"

She nodded. "The first round missed him. I thought he would run away. Instead, he turned on me with the knife. When he lunged, I fired. The round hit him in the chest."

"That's a heavy load you've had to carry, Kelly."

She licked her lips. "My mother and I never talked about what happened. I…I always thought she hated me because I'd taken him from her."

"But that can't be true, Kelly."

"I realize it now. She told one of the nurses at Magnolia Gardens that I was a good daughter."

Kelly swallowed down the lump that filled her throat. "All I ever wanted was a normal home and loving parents. I never admitted it to anyone, not even myself, but I loved my dad. More than anything, I wanted him to love me."

"Oh, honey." Phil scooted next to her and pulled her into his arms.

"In the end, my dad thought more of the drugs he took

than either mom or me." Tears stung her eyes. "I didn't have a choice that night. If I hadn't stopped him, he...he would have killed both of us."

"That's why you're so determined to be an ace shot."

She nodded.

"But good came from what happened." Phil put his finger under her chin. "Do you know why?"

She shook her head.

"That sharp-shooter ability of yours saved my life." Phil pulled her deeper into his arms. "I love you, Kelly."

She melted into his welcoming embrace. "Oh, Phil, I love you, too."

Feeling the strength of his hold and the steady thump of his heart, Kelly knew that the past was behind her. At long last, she had come home to a man who would love her and cherish her for the rest of her life.

TWENTY-FIVE

Kelly slid into the pew next to Phil on Sunday morning and grabbed his bandaged arm. Private Stanley sat a few rows ahead of them, his Bible open, his eyes closed.

"He's going to be okay," Phil whispered. "Thanks to you."

"Include yourself in that. Chief Agent in Charge Wilson said we both did a good job."

Phil squeezed her hand, taking care not to hurt the cuts that were starting to mend. "The Chief is proud of you, Kelly. So am I."

Her cheeks warmed with the praise. "Mrs. Foglio says she wants to help Kyle any way she can. I'm not sure what will happen."

"Sergeant Meyers and his wife told me the same thing." Phil rubbed his fingers over her arm. "Did you see Mildred?"

Kelly nodded. "She's back at Magnolia Gardens and gaining strength. They found her brother's body and Lola admitted she and Gates killed him, never realizing Mildred owned both pieces of land. If that housing deal goes through, Millie will be a wealthy lady and wants to use some of her money to help with Kyle's rehabilitation."

"Maybe he'll make it after all." Phil leaned closer. "I called Aunt Eleanor and thanked her for keeping me on the straight and narrow."

"I'd like to meet her someday."

"The feeling's mutual."

Kelly's heart skipped a beat. "You mentioned me?"

His eyes twinkled. "I told her I'd found someone special."

The organ began to play. Chaplain Sanchez entered the sanctuary, and the congregation stood. Kelly gazed up at Phil, dreaming of a day in the not-too-distant future when she would be standing next to him at the altar in this very church. *Oh, Lord, if only that could be.*

After the service, they chatted briefly with the chaplain and then stepped into the warmth of the sunny fall day. "There's a path that cuts through the trees and heads to a pond." Phil pointed to where the pavement disappeared into the woods.

Hand in hand they strolled, enjoying the rich colors of the leaves and the unseasonably mild temperature. When they got to the secluded pond, Phil stopped and pulled in a deep lungful of air. Concern tingled Kelly's neck as she realized a problem was weighing heavy on his mind.

He released her hand. "There's something we need to discuss before we go any farther. I've got another year at Fort Rickman before the next assignment. Then I'll have to move wherever Uncle Sam sends me."

Her pulse quickened with apprehension.

"Your career is just as important as mine, Kelly. I would never stand in your way for promotion, which means you'll have to accept future assignments no matter where they might take you or how far apart we might be."

Did Phil want to say goodbye? Then she looked into his eyes and read something completely different in his gaze.

He stepped closer. "As far as I'm concerned, we can work through the separations."

Letting out the breath she had been holding, Kelly reached

for his hand and wove her fingers through his. "Although I love the military and what I do, it's a job, Phil."

Her cheeks burned. Hopefully she wasn't saying too much, but the issue of both of them being in the military needed to be addressed so they could move forward. Although many couples made their marriages work when both spouses were in uniform, Kelly didn't want the long-term separations that seemed inevitable when two careers were on the line.

"A man and woman need to weigh what's best for them as a couple, and…" She hesitated. "If they marry, they need to consider any children they might have. My mom was never there for me. I don't want that for my kids."

His brow furrowed. "But…but what about your career?"

"We'll deal with that when the time comes. If you get reassigned and the army isn't willing to assign me to the same post, then we'll have to make a decision about whether I stay in the service."

She wrapped her arms around his neck. "Just to let you know where I stand, family always comes first."

A wide smile covered his face. "I like the sound of that."

Kelly tilted her head. "The sound of what?"

"Family." He drew her closer and kissed her forehead. Then, pulling back ever so slightly, he gazed into her eyes. "I'm probably jumping the gun, but how do you feel about a trip to New Orleans? I've never been back since my dad was thrown in jail."

"And I've never been at all."

"So—" Phil raised his brow.

Kelly smiled. "In my opinion, spring will be a perfect time to see New Orleans."

He rubbed his hand along her cheek. "Should we ask Chaplain Sanchez to save a date for us here in either April or May?"

Without saying anything specific, they had decided everything. A spring wedding and a honeymoon in New Orleans.

"I do," she whispered, practicing her line.

He leaned closer. "What's that?"

"I do love you, Jean Philippe Thibodeaux."

"Not as much as I love you, Kelly McQueen."

"Laissez les bon temps rouler." She laughed with joy. "Let the good times roll."

Phil's eyes held the promise of the wonderful life they would share together. "Every day will be a good day if I'm with you."

Stepping even closer to her handsome Cajun, Kelly molded into his arms and lifted her lips to his. God had healed their broken pasts and given them a future full of love. Phil's kiss was long and lingering, and Kelly knew without a shadow of a doubt she wanted to be wrapped in his love for the rest of her life.

* * * * *

Dear Reader,

I hope you enjoy *The Captain's Mission,* book two in my Military Investigations series. The story deals with the importance of family and especially the role fathers play in their children's lives. In my writing, I often explore how hurts in the past hold us back in the present and keep us from being free to embrace the future.

U.S. Army CID Special Agent Kelly McQueen and Captain Phil Thibodeaux have a lot to uncover about their pasts. Working together as they investigate a training accident at Fort Rickman, Georgia, Kelly and Phil learn about love and acceptance and the healing power of God's forgiveness.

I hope you've experienced God's healing, whether physical, emotional or spiritual. If you're still troubled by unresolved problems, turn to the Lord in your need and ask Him to lift the burdens from your heart.

I always enjoy hearing from my readers. Write to me c/o Love Inspired, 233 Broadway, Suite 1001, New York, NY 10279. Visit me online at www.DebbyGiusti.com, blog with me at www.seekerville.blogspot.com and join my Prayer Team at www.crossmyheartprayerteam.blogspot.com. Watch for the next exciting book in my series, coming soon to a bookstore near you.

Wishing you abundant blessings,

Debby Giusti

Questions for Discussion

1. Why did Phil not want to get involved with Kelly at the beginning of the story? How did his feelings toward his own mother influence his relationship with Kelly?

2. Why was the teacup collection important to Kelly?

3. Military communities often welcome newcomers and say goodbye to those who are moving to new duty stations at monthly social gatherings called Hail and Farewells. How do you greet the newly arrived in your neighborhood, church or work environment? Do you say goodbye in a special way?

4. Compare and contrast Kelly's mother with Phil's. Which woman seemed to be a more loving mother?

5. Compare the two fathers. What type of father will Phil be when he and Kelly have children?

6. Do you understand Kelly's hesitancy to return to Magnolia Gardens? Has fear ever kept you from reaching out to others?

7. Disappointments and pain in the past can keep us from living fully in the present. How was that revealed in this story?

8. Why was Kelly relieved when she saw the new resident in her mother's old room at Magnolia Gardens? How would you feel in that situation?

9. When a military service member dies, a survival assistance officer is assigned to help the spouse and family. What happens in your community or church when someone dies? In what way do you reach out to those who are grieving?

10. Scripture assures us that with God all things work for good. How is that revealed in Kelly's life?

11. How does Officer Simpson's statement, "The apple never falls far from the tree," affect Phil and Kelly? Do you think the cliché holds true? What about in Kyle's case?

12. What do you think will happen to Kyle?

13. Who reached out to Phil when he was young and how did their influence impact his life?

14. Can a lone voice of reason sway people in a positive way? How did Phil bring the crowd to their senses at the campsite?

15. What did you learn from this story?

INSPIRATIONAL

Inspirational romances to warm your heart & soul.

SUSPENSE

TITLES AVAILABLE NEXT MONTH

Available November 8, 2011

PRIVATE EYE PROTECTOR
Heroes for Hire
Shirlee McCoy

PROOF OF LIFE
Laura Scott

CHRISTMAS HAVEN
Hope White

BOUNTY HUNTER GUARDIAN
Diane Burke

LISCNM1011

REQUEST YOUR FREE BOOKS!
2 FREE RIVETING INSPIRATIONAL NOVELS
PLUS 2 FREE MYSTERY GIFTS

Love Inspired®
SUSPENSE

YES! Please send me 2 FREE Love Inspired® Suspense novels and my 2 FREE mystery gifts (gifts are worth about $10). After receiving them, if I don't wish to receive any more books, I can return the shipping statement marked "cancel". If I don't cancel, I will receive 4 brand-new novels every month and be billed just $4.49 per book in the U.S. or $4.99 per book in Canada. That's a saving of at least 22% off the cover price. It's quite a bargain! Shipping and handling is just 50¢ per book in the U.S. and 75¢ per book in Canada.* I understand that accepting the 2 free books and gifts places me under no obligation to buy anything. I can always return a shipment and cancel at any time. Even if I never buy another book, the two free books and gifts are mine to keep forever.

123/323 IDN FEHR

Name	(PLEASE PRINT)	
Address		Apt. #
City	State/Prov.	Zip/Postal Code

Signature (if under 18, a parent or guardian must sign)

Mail to the **Reader Service:**
IN U.S.A.: P.O. Box 1867, Buffalo, NY 14240-1867
IN CANADA: P.O. Box 609, Fort Erie, Ontario L2A 5X3

Not valid for current subscribers to Love Inspired Suspense books.

**Are you a subscriber to Love Inspired Suspense
and want to receive the larger-print edition?
Call 1-800-873-8635 or visit www.ReaderService.com.**

* Terms and prices subject to change without notice. Prices do not include applicable taxes. Sales tax applicable in N.Y. Canadian residents will be charged applicable taxes. Offer not valid in Quebec. This offer is limited to one order per household. All orders subject to credit approval. Credit or debit balances in a customer's account(s) may be offset by any other outstanding balance owed by or to the customer. Please allow 4 to 6 weeks for delivery. Offer available while quantities last.

Your Privacy—The Reader Service is committed to protecting your privacy. Our Privacy Policy is available online at www.ReaderService.com or upon request from the Reader Service.

We make a portion of our mailing list available to reputable third parties that offer products we believe may interest you. If you prefer that we not exchange your name with third parties, or if you wish to clarify or modify your communication preferences, please visit us at www.ReaderService.com/consumerschoice or write to us at Reader Service Preference Service, P.O. Box 9062, Buffalo, NY 14269. Include your complete name and address.

LISUS11B

Rodeo rider Wade Stone never thought he'd step foot in Dry Creek, Montana, again. But nine years later, he's back on Stone ranch, getting stared down by the townspeople. All *except* Amy Mitchell, whose heart he broke. With everyone against them, surely there's no second chance for this couple….

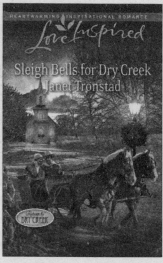

Sleigh Bells for Dry Creek

by Janet Tronstad

www.LoveInspiredBooks.com

LI87703